The Political Assassin

Political, Volume 1

Nicholas Andrew Martinez

Published by Harmony House Publishing, 2024.

This is a work of fiction. Similarities to real people, places, or events are entirely coincidental.

THE POLITICAL ASSASSIN

First edition. November 24, 2024.

Copyright © 2024 Nicholas Andrew Martinez.

ISBN: 979-8230642718

Written by Nicholas Andrew Martinez.

Table of Contents

Chapter 1: Shadows of Power 1
Chapter 2: The First Strike 5
Chapter 3: Unseen Threats 12
Chapter 4: The Governor's Gambit 19
Chapter 5: Web of Deceit 30
Chapter 6: A Dangerous Game 36
Chapter 7: The Puppet Masters 42
Chapter 8: The General's Fall 50
Chapter 9: Crossroads 61
Chapter 10: The Financial Web 66
Chapter 11: Allies and Adversaries 73
Chapter 12: The Senator's Secret 83
Chapter 13: The Final Target 89
Chapter 14: The Reckoning 94
Chapter 15: A New Dawn 101

To those who fight for truth in the shadows,

To the brave souls who dare to expose corruption,

And to the relentless seekers of justice,

This story is for you.

Chapter 1: Shadows of Power

In the heart of the city, where the sky was perpetually darkened by the smoke of industry and the whispers of corruption, Alex Morgan moved through the streets of Veridan with the ease of a ghost. His tall, lean frame was cloaked in the anonymity of the night, blending seamlessly into the urban landscape. The air was thick with the stench of decay and the tension of a society on the brink of collapse. Veridan, once a beacon of hope and prosperity, was now a land of shadows and power plays, a chessboard where the pawns rarely survived.

Alex's footsteps were silent as he navigated the narrow alleyways, his senses heightened by years of military training. His sharp blue eyes, once filled with the idealism of youth, now held the cold calculation of a seasoned operative. He had been many things in his life: a son, a soldier, a patriot. Now, he was something entirely different—a political assassin, a weapon forged by the fires of betrayal and loss.

The city of Veridan was a stark contrast to the life Alex had known in his youth. He had grown up in the tranquil countryside, in a small village where everyone knew each other, and the air was clean and filled with the scent of wildflowers. His father had been a farmer, his mother a schoolteacher. They had instilled in him a strong sense of duty and justice, values that had led him to join the military at the age of eighteen. He had served with distinction, rising through the ranks to become a highly respected officer.

But war changes people. The things Alex had seen and done in the name of his country had left scars, both visible and invisible. The turning point had come during a mission in a distant land, a mission that had gone horribly wrong. Betrayed by those he trusted, Alex had watched helplessly as his comrades were slaughtered. He had barely escaped with his life, but the man who returned to Veridan was not the same. Disillusioned and embittered, he had left the military, severing ties with the life he had once known.

The transition from soldier to assassin had not been a straightforward one. It had begun with a chance encounter in a seedy bar on the outskirts of the city. Alex had been drowning his sorrows, contemplating the emptiness of his future, when a man had approached him with an offer. The man, known only as "The Handler," had an air of authority and mystery. He had spoken of a higher purpose, a way to make a difference in a world gone mad. Desperate for direction, Alex had agreed, and thus began his new life in the shadows.

As he moved through the city, Alex's mind drifted to his latest mission. The target was Senator James Caldwell, a prominent political figure known for his fiery speeches and populist rhetoric. Caldwell had risen to power on the back of a discontented populace, promising change and justice. But Alex knew better. He had seen the reports, the classified documents that revealed Caldwell's true nature—a man driven by ambition, willing to sacrifice anything and anyone for his own gain.

Alex's destination was a run-down apartment building on the outskirts of the city. It was one of his safe houses, a place where he could plan and prepare without fear of discovery. He slipped through the back entrance, making his way up the creaking stairs to the third floor. Inside the apartment, he activated a series of security measures, ensuring that he was alone and undisturbed.

The room was sparsely furnished, with only the essentials. A cot in the corner, a small table and chair, and a series of monitors and communication devices. Alex sat down at the table, pulling out a folder marked with the insignia of The Handler. Inside were detailed profiles and intelligence reports on Senator Caldwell. Alex began to read, his mind absorbing the information with the precision of a machine.

Caldwell's rise to power had been meteoric. He had started as a lawyer, championing the causes of the underprivileged and marginalized. His fiery oratory skills and charisma had won him a loyal following, and he had quickly ascended the political ladder. But behind the facade of the people's champion was a man who thrived on chaos and division. Caldwell had manipulated the fears and frustrations of the populace, turning them against each other for his own benefit.

Alex's mission was clear: Caldwell had to be eliminated. The senator's influence was growing, and his plans threatened to plunge Veridan into further turmoil. But this was not just about politics; it was personal. The Handler had made it clear that Caldwell was responsible for the betrayal that had led to the massacre of Alex's unit. The man who had once been a hero to the people was nothing more than a puppet master, pulling the strings from the shadows.

As Alex read through the dossier, his mind began to formulate a plan. Caldwell was a careful man, always surrounded by security. The assassination would require precision and cunning, exploiting any weaknesses in the senator's routine. Alex noted Caldwell's upcoming schedule, pinpointing a charity gala where the senator would be in attendance. It was a high-profile event, perfect for making a statement.

The plan began to take shape in Alex's mind. He would need to gain access to the gala, posing as one of the many service staff. From there, he could get close to Caldwell, ensuring that the hit was clean and untraceable. It was a risky move, but Alex thrived on risk. It was what made him the best at what he did.

Days turned into nights as Alex prepared for the mission. He gathered the necessary equipment, studied the floor plans of the gala venue, and rehearsed his every move. There was no room for error. Each step had to be executed with military precision. As the night of the gala approached, Alex felt the familiar adrenaline coursing through his veins. This was his element, the calm before the storm.

On the night of the gala, the city of Veridan was alive with lights and festivities. The wealthy and powerful gathered in their finest attire, oblivious to the danger that lurked in their midst. Alex, dressed as a waiter, moved through the crowd with practiced ease. His sharp eyes scanned the room, locating Caldwell surrounded by his entourage.

As he approached the senator, Alex's mind was focused and clear. He reached into his pocket, feeling the cold metal of the syringe. The poison was fast-acting and undetectable, ensuring that Caldwell's death would appear as a natural heart attack. With practiced ease, Alex made his way to Caldwell, offering him a glass of champagne.

The moment was perfect, a brief exchange of pleasantries, a subtle prick of the syringe, and it was done. Caldwell would be dead within minutes, his bodyguards none the wiser. Alex moved away, blending back into the crowd, his mission complete. He exited the venue, disappearing into the night as the chaos began to unfold behind him.

Back in his safe house, Alex monitored the news. Reports of Caldwell's sudden death dominated the headlines, speculation rife about the implications for Veridan's political future. But for Alex, it was just another mission, another step in the long journey of retribution. He knew that The Handler would be contacting him soon with new orders, a new target. The cycle would continue, the shadows growing darker with each passing day.

As he sat in the dimly lit room, Alex allowed himself a moment of reflection. The life he had chosen was a lonely one, filled with danger and uncertainty. But it was also a life of purpose, a way to right the wrongs that had been done to him and his comrades. He had become a weapon, honed and deadly, in the service of a higher cause.

In the distance, the city of Veridan continued to pulse with life, a sprawling metropolis of power and corruption. Alex knew that as long as men like Caldwell existed, there would be a need for someone like him. A guardian in the shadows, an assassin with a conscience, driven by a desire for justice and vengeance. The path he walked was a dark one, but it was a path he had chosen willingly, and he would follow it to the end.

The next morning, as the first light of dawn broke over the city, Alex received a message on his secure line. The Handler had a new mission for him, a new target to eliminate. Alex read the details, his mind already shifting into gear. The hunt was on once more, and the shadows of power would tremble in his wake.

Chapter 2: The First Strike

The gala night that marked the end of Senator Caldwell's life had passed into history as a turning point for the nation of Veridan. The assassination had been a flawless execution, a testament to Alex Morgan's meticulous planning and lethal efficiency. The aftermath, however, was a storm that rocked the very foundations of the political landscape.

As the city of Veridan awoke to the news of Caldwell's sudden death, the airwaves buzzed with shock and speculation. Newscasters reported live from the scene, their voices a blend of disbelief and urgency. Political analysts scrambled to make sense of the event, while ordinary citizens watched in stunned silence, grappling with the implications for their future.

Alex Morgan, the man behind the chaos, was already several steps ahead. From the safety of his nondescript apartment, he monitored the fallout with cold detachment. His mission had been successful, but his work was far from over. The next phase required careful observation and analysis, a keen understanding of the shifting dynamics in Veridan's political arena.

The days following the assassination were a blur of activity. The media frenzy reached a fever pitch as journalists dug into Caldwell's background, uncovering both his achievements and his controversies. Conspiracy theories flourished, some pointing to rival politicians, others to shadowy organizations with hidden agendas. In this maelstrom, the true story—Alex's story—remained hidden, buried beneath layers of speculation and intrigue.

At the heart of the chaos was The Handler, the enigmatic figure who had orchestrated the assassination. To Alex, The Handler was both a benefactor and a mystery. Their communications were brief, encrypted, and devoid of personal details. All Alex knew was that The Handler had resources and intelligence far beyond his own, and a seemingly unerring sense of who needed to be eliminated to achieve a greater purpose.

The morning after Caldwell's death, Alex received a new message from The Handler. It arrived through their usual secure channel, a brief text that appeared on his screen:

"Mission accomplished. Next target: Deputy Prime Minister, Richard Hawke. Details to follow."

Alex read the message, committing it to memory before it disappeared from the screen. Richard Hawke, the Deputy Prime Minister, was a significant escalation. Taking down such a high-ranking official would send shockwaves through the government and potentially destabilize the entire administration. It was a bold move, but one that fit the pattern of The Handler's strategy: create chaos to expose corruption.

The first step in planning the assassination was gathering intelligence. Alex knew that Hawke was a seasoned politician, a man with a reputation for being shrewd and ruthless. He would be heavily guarded, his movements carefully monitored. To succeed, Alex needed to learn everything about his target's routine, security measures, and potential vulnerabilities.

Over the next few days, Alex immersed himself in research. He hacked into government databases, sifted through news articles, and tapped into underground networks of informants. Every piece of information was meticulously cataloged, forming a comprehensive profile of Richard Hawke.

Hawke's daily schedule was predictable, a testament to his disciplined nature. He attended regular meetings at the Prime Minister's office, held press conferences, and participated in high-profile events. His security detail was tight, a combination of government bodyguards and private contractors. There were few opportunities to strike, but Alex was patient. He knew that even the most fortified defenses had weaknesses.

The breakthrough came when Alex discovered that Hawke was scheduled to attend a private fundraiser at an exclusive country club. The event was invitation-only, with a guest list that included some of Veridan's most influential figures. It was the perfect setting for an assassination: a controlled environment with limited security compared to the public venues Hawke usually frequented.

With the target and location identified, Alex began to devise his plan. The first challenge was gaining access to the country club. He needed an identity that would allow him to move freely among the guests, someone who wouldn't arouse suspicion. After careful consideration, he settled on the persona of a high-end caterer. It was a role that provided the perfect cover: access to all areas, minimal scrutiny, and the ability to carry necessary equipment without raising alarms.

Securing the necessary credentials required a combination of bribery and forgery. Alex reached out to his network of contacts, acquiring the documents and uniforms needed to blend in with the catering staff. He practiced his role, learning the layout of the club, the timing of the event, and the movements of the staff. Every detail was rehearsed until it became second nature.

The day of the fundraiser arrived, and Alex executed his plan with precision. Dressed in the uniform of a caterer, he arrived at the country club hours before the event began. He moved through the kitchen and service areas, familiarizing himself with the layout and establishing his presence. His calm demeanor and practiced efficiency drew no undue attention from the other staff or security personnel.

As the guests began to arrive, Alex took his position, serving drinks and appetizers while keeping a watchful eye on his target. Hawke arrived with his usual entourage, a small group of bodyguards who remained close but unobtrusive. The Deputy Prime Minister mingled with the guests, his charm and charisma on full display. To the casual observer, it was just another social event, but to Alex, it was the culmination of days of planning.

The opportunity came during the dinner service. Hawke was seated at the head table, engaged in conversation with a group of influential donors. Alex approached with a tray of drinks, his movements smooth and unremarkable. As he set down a glass in front of Hawke, he slipped a small vial into the wine, a potent poison that would cause a fatal heart attack within minutes.

Hawke took the glass, raising it in a toast to his companions. Alex watched from a distance, his heart pounding with anticipation. The poison worked quickly, and within moments, Hawke's face turned pale. He clutched his chest, gasping for breath as he collapsed. The room erupted in panic, guests and security rushing to his aid, but it was too late. The Deputy Prime Minister was dead.

Amid the chaos, Alex slipped away, blending into the crowd of fleeing guests. He exited the country club through a side door, disappearing into the night as the sirens of approaching ambulances filled the air. The mission was complete, but the true impact was yet to be felt.

The assassination of Richard Hawke sent shockwaves through Veridan's political landscape. The government declared a state of emergency, launching a full-scale investigation into the deaths of both Caldwell and Hawke. Security was tightened, and the public was gripped by fear and uncertainty. Conspiracy theories flourished, with accusations flying between rival political factions.

Key political players emerged from the shadows, each with their own agendas and reactions to the assassinations. Prime Minister Eleanor Wexler, a seasoned politician with a reputation for pragmatism, addressed the nation in a televised speech. She called for unity and calm, vowing to bring those responsible to justice. Her demeanor was composed, but behind the scenes, she was deeply concerned about the stability of her administration.

Opposition leader Thomas Redmond, a fiery populist with a knack for stirring public sentiment, seized the opportunity to criticize the government. He accused Wexler's administration of incompetence and corruption, promising to restore order and transparency. Redmond's rhetoric resonated with a disillusioned populace, further polarizing the political climate.

In the midst of the turmoil, Alex received another message from The Handler. This time, it was a voice message, delivered through a secure channel. The voice was distorted, unrecognizable, but the message was clear:

"Well done, Alex. The first strike has been successful. The government is reeling, and our true enemies are beginning to show themselves. Your next target is Minister of Defense, Victor Lang. Details will follow."

Victor Lang, the Minister of Defense, was a formidable adversary. A former general with a reputation for ruthlessness, he was known for his iron-fisted approach to security and his close ties to the military-industrial complex. Taking him down would require a different strategy, one that exploited his weaknesses and circumvented his formidable defenses.

As Alex began to gather intelligence on Lang, he couldn't help but reflect on the path that had brought him to this point. He had become a tool in a larger game, a pawn in the hands of The Handler. But he also understood the necessity of his actions. The corruption and deceit that permeated Veridan's government needed to be exposed, and sometimes, the only way to do that was through drastic measures.

Over the next few days, Alex's research into Lang's background and routine yielded valuable insights. Lang was a creature of habit, his movements and schedule highly predictable. He lived in a heavily fortified mansion, surrounded by security, but he also had a weakness: a penchant for high-stakes gambling. Lang frequented an exclusive underground casino, a place where the wealthy and powerful indulged their vices away from the public eye.

The casino, known as "The Den," was the key to Alex's plan. It was a place where Lang let his guard down, surrounded by opulence and vice. Alex decided to infiltrate the casino, posing as a high roller to gain access to Lang. It was a risky move, but it provided the best opportunity to get close to the Minister of Defense.

Securing an invitation to The Den required pulling strings and leveraging contacts. Alex reached out to his network, using his resources to create a convincing cover story. He assumed the identity of "Lucas Drake," a wealthy businessman with a taste for high-stakes gambling. The necessary credentials were forged, and Alex practiced his role until he could slip into character effortlessly.

The night of the infiltration arrived, and Alex made his way to The Den, a lavish establishment hidden beneath the facade of a legitimate business. The entrance was discreet, guarded by men who checked his credentials before granting him access. Inside, the casino was a world of luxury and excess, with ornate chandeliers, plush carpets, and the sound of clinking glasses and shuffled cards filling the air.

Alex moved through the crowd, his demeanor that of a confident gambler. He located Lang at a private table, surrounded by a group of similarly powerful individuals. Lang was engrossed in a game of poker, his attention focused on the cards and the sizable stack of chips in front of him. Alex watched, biding his time, waiting for the right moment to make his move.

As the night progressed, Alex positioned himself at a nearby table, engaging in his own game and winning steadily. His reputation as a skilled gambler quickly spread, drawing the attention of other players and spectators. Eventually, Lang took notice, intrigued by the new player who seemed to be on a winning streak.

Alex capitalized on this curiosity, making a bold bet that caught Lang's attention. The stakes were high, and the tension in the room palpable as the cards were dealt. Alex played his hand with calculated precision, using his skills to outmaneuver Lang and win the pot. Lang, impressed and intrigued, invited Alex to join his table for the next round.

The two men exchanged introductions, Lang unaware of Alex's true identity. They played several rounds, with Alex deliberately losing a few hands to maintain the illusion of chance. Throughout the game, Alex subtly probed Lang, gathering information and assessing his target's demeanor. Lang was confident, almost arrogant, his guard lowered in the familiar surroundings of The Den.

The opportunity to strike came when Lang excused himself to visit a private room, a secluded area reserved for VIP guests. Alex followed at a discreet distance, his heart pounding with anticipation. He waited until Lang was alone, then made his move.

The confrontation was swift and silent. Alex approached from behind, a garrote wire in hand. He looped it around Lang's neck, tightening it with practiced efficiency. Lang struggled, his hands clawing at the wire, but the fight was brief. Within moments, the Minister of Defense was dead, his body slumped in the opulent room.

Alex quickly searched Lang's pockets, retrieving a keycard and a small notebook. The keycard provided access to Lang's personal office, a treasure trove of classified information that could prove invaluable. The notebook contained cryptic notes and contacts, a glimpse into the network of power and corruption that Lang was a part of.

Leaving the room, Alex made his way out of The Den, maintaining his cover until he was safely away from the casino. The mission had been a success, but the implications of Lang's death were far-reaching. The government of Veridan was in turmoil, and the balance of power was shifting in unpredictable ways.

Back in his apartment, Alex reviewed the contents of the notebook, piecing together the connections and alliances that Lang had cultivated. The names and codes hinted at a deeper conspiracy, one that extended beyond Veridan's borders. The Handler's strategy was becoming clearer: disrupt the existing power structure to expose the hidden forces that truly controlled the nation.

As he prepared to send his findings to The Handler, Alex couldn't shake the feeling that he was part of something much larger, a game with stakes higher than he had ever imagined. The path he walked was a dangerous one, but he was committed to seeing it through, driven by a sense of justice and a desire for retribution.

The message to The Handler was brief, detailing the success of the mission and the information obtained. Alex sent it through their secure channel, waiting for the response. It came within minutes, a voice message that conveyed a sense of satisfaction and anticipation:

"Excellent work, Alex. Lang's death will send a clear message. Our enemies are beginning to show their true faces. Your next target is Prime Minister Eleanor Wexler. This will be the most challenging mission yet, but it is essential for our cause. Details to follow."

Alex's heart skipped a beat at the mention of Wexler. Taking down the Prime Minister was a daunting task, one that would require unparalleled precision and planning. But he understood the significance. Wexler's removal would create a power vacuum, forcing the hidden forces to reveal themselves and allowing The Handler's true plan to unfold.

As he began to prepare for the next mission, Alex couldn't help but wonder about The Handler's identity and ultimate goal. The enigmatic figure had proven to be a master strategist, but their true motives remained shrouded in mystery. For now, Alex focused on the task at hand, knowing that the answers would come in time.

The political landscape of Veridan was shifting, and the shadows of power were growing darker. Alex Morgan, the political assassin, was at the center of it all, a force of change in a world teetering on the edge of chaos. The first strike had been made, but the battle was far from over. As he moved forward, Alex knew that each mission brought him closer to the truth, and to the reckoning that awaited in the shadows.

Chapter 3: Unseen Threats

The city of Veridan lay in a state of uneasy tension, its political landscape reeling from the shockwaves of recent events. The assassinations of Senator James Caldwell and Deputy Prime Minister Richard Hawke had plunged the government into chaos, triggering a desperate search for answers and stability. Amidst this turmoil, Alex Morgan moved like a phantom, his every step a calculated maneuver in a deadly game of shadows and power.

In the wake of Hawke's assassination, the government had launched a full-scale manhunt for the mysterious assassin responsible for the high-profile killings. Security measures were heightened, and a special task force was formed, led by one of Veridan's most relentless investigators, Inspector Samuel Carr. Known for his dogged determination and keen intellect, Carr was a formidable adversary, a man who would stop at nothing to uncover the truth.

For Alex, the increased scrutiny meant adopting even greater caution. He had become adept at evading detection, using a combination of technological savvy and old-fashioned tradecraft. But the stakes were higher now, and any misstep could lead to his capture or death. As he navigated the labyrinthine streets of Veridan, Alex's mind was focused on his next objective: Governor Evelyn Price.

Price was a significant figure in Veridan's political hierarchy, a governor with a reputation for ruthlessness and corruption. Her influence extended beyond the political realm, intertwining with powerful corporate interests that thrived on exploitation and deceit. Targeting her would not only disrupt the existing power structure but also expose the hidden alliances that fueled Veridan's descent into darkness.

To understand the full extent of Price's operations, Alex needed to delve deeper into the political underbelly of Veridan. He began by infiltrating the networks of informants and operatives that thrived in the city's shadows. These were individuals who traded in secrets and information, their loyalty bought and sold like any other commodity. Alex used his connections to gain access to the inner workings of Price's administration, piecing together a complex web of deceit and manipulation.

The more he uncovered, the clearer it became that Price was not acting alone. She was part of a larger conspiracy, a coalition of high-ranking officials and powerful corporations that wielded their influence from the shadows. This cabal had its tentacles in every aspect of Veridan's society, from the halls of government to the boardrooms of multinational conglomerates. Their goal was simple: to consolidate power and wealth at the expense of the people.

Alex's investigation led him to a series of clandestine meetings held in the most unexpected places: an abandoned warehouse on the outskirts of the city, a luxurious penthouse in the financial district, and even a secluded country estate far from prying eyes. Each location revealed a new piece of the puzzle, a deeper layer of the conspiracy that had ensnared Veridan in its grasp.

One of the most significant revelations came from a former associate of Price, a disgraced politician named Marcus Dyer. Dyer had been ousted from power after a scandal, but he still harbored valuable information about Price's operations. Alex tracked him down to a rundown apartment in the city's slums, a place where Dyer lived in squalor, haunted by his past.

Dyer was initially reluctant to talk, fearing retribution from Price and her allies. But Alex's persistence and a promise of protection eventually persuaded him to share what he knew. Dyer revealed that Price had been involved in a series of illegal deals with powerful corporations, exchanging political favors for financial backing. These corporations, in turn, used their influence to manipulate policies and regulations to their advantage, creating a symbiotic relationship that enriched both parties.

The most damning piece of information, however, was the existence of a secret document, known as the "Veridan Accord." This document outlined the terms of the alliance between Price and her corporate backers, detailing their plans to privatize essential public services, exploit natural resources, and undermine democratic institutions. The Accord was the blueprint for their domination, a testament to their greed and ambition.

Obtaining the Veridan Accord became Alex's top priority. He knew that exposing the document would be a devastating blow to Price and her allies, providing irrefutable evidence of their corruption. But the Accord was heavily guarded, kept in a secure vault within Price's personal residence—a sprawling mansion fortified with state-of-the-art security systems and a contingent of loyal guards.

Alex began to plan the operation with his characteristic precision. He conducted reconnaissance on the mansion, mapping out its defenses and identifying potential entry points. He acquired the necessary equipment, including high-tech gadgets to bypass security systems and weapons for neutralizing guards if necessary. Every detail was considered, every contingency accounted for.

The night of the operation arrived, and Alex made his way to the mansion under the cover of darkness. He approached from the rear, avoiding the main entrance and the patrolling guards. Using a grappling hook, he scaled the high walls and landed silently in the garden. From there, he moved with the stealth of a predator, his senses attuned to every sound and movement.

The first obstacle was the perimeter alarm system, a sophisticated network of sensors and cameras designed to detect intruders. Alex used a jammer to disable the sensors temporarily, creating a window of opportunity to slip past undetected. He then made his way to a side entrance, picking the lock with practiced ease.

Inside the mansion, Alex navigated the dimly lit corridors, his footsteps silent on the plush carpets. He encountered several guards along the way, dispatching them with a combination of hand-to-hand combat and tranquilizer darts. His movements were fluid and precise, a testament to his training and experience.

The vault was located in Price's private study, a room adorned with opulent furnishings and priceless artwork. Alex approached the heavy metal door, examining the biometric lock that secured it. He retrieved a device from his backpack, a sophisticated tool designed to hack biometric systems. Within minutes, the lock disengaged, and the door swung open.

Inside the vault, Alex found the Veridan Accord, a thick document bound in leather. He quickly scanned its contents, confirming the extent of the conspiracy. The Accord was a damning indictment of Price and her allies, a testament to their treachery and greed. Alex took photographs of the document, ensuring he had multiple copies as evidence.

As he prepared to leave, Alex heard the sound of approaching footsteps. He ducked behind a bookshelf, his hand instinctively reaching for his weapon.

A guard entered the study, his flashlight sweeping the room. Alex waited, his muscles tense, until the guard turned his back. With a swift and silent move, he incapacitated the guard, ensuring his presence remained undetected.

Alex exited the mansion the same way he had entered, using the jammer to disable the perimeter alarms once more. He scaled the walls and disappeared into the night, the Veridan Accord safely in his possession. The operation had been a success, but the real battle was just beginning.

The following day, Alex contacted The Handler, sending the photographs of the Veridan Accord through their secure channel. The response was swift and concise:

"Excellent work, Alex. The Accord is the key to exposing Price and her allies. Prepare for the next phase. Your new target is Governor Evelyn Price. Details to follow."

The assassination of Price would be the culmination of Alex's mission, the final blow against the corrupt alliance that had ensnared Veridan. But it was also the most dangerous part of the operation. Price was a high-profile target, and her death would provoke a fierce response from her allies and the government.

As Alex prepared for the mission, tensions continued to rise in Veridan. The manhunt for Caldwell's assassin intensified, with Inspector Carr closing in on potential suspects. The media frenzy showed no signs of abating, and public anger reached a boiling point. Protests erupted in the streets, demanding justice and accountability from the government.

Amidst this turmoil, Alex maintained his focus, his mind clear and resolute. He had chosen this path, and he would see it through to the end. The shadows of power were vast and formidable, but Alex was determined to bring them into the light, no matter the cost.

Governor Evelyn Price was a formidable adversary, a woman who had risen to power through cunning and ruthlessness. She had built her empire on a foundation of deceit and manipulation, using her political influence to enrich herself and her corporate backers. But beneath her veneer of respectability, Price was deeply corrupt, her hands stained with the suffering of countless individuals.

To eliminate Price, Alex needed to find a way to get close to her. He began by studying her schedule, looking for any vulnerabilities or opportunities. Price was highly guarded, with a security detail that rivaled that of the Prime Minister. She rarely ventured out in public without a contingent of bodyguards, and her mansion was a fortress.

The breakthrough came when Alex discovered that Price had a secret lover, a young socialite named Rebecca who frequented the city's elite circles. Price's relationship with Rebecca was kept hidden from the public, a scandalous affair that could damage her carefully crafted image. Alex saw this as an opportunity to exploit.

Using his network of contacts, Alex gathered information about Rebecca's habits and routines. He learned that she often visited a luxurious spa in the heart of the city, a place where Veridan's wealthy and powerful went to unwind and indulge. Alex decided to use this information to his advantage.

He approached Rebecca one evening as she left the spa, presenting himself as a concerned friend. He had carefully crafted a cover story, posing as a private investigator who had uncovered evidence of Price's corruption. He showed Rebecca the photographs of the Veridan Accord, playing on her emotions and fears.

Rebecca was initially skeptical, but Alex's calm demeanor and the compelling evidence swayed her. She agreed to help him, providing him with details about Price's movements and schedule. In return, Alex promised to protect her and ensure that Price's crimes were exposed

.

With Rebecca's assistance, Alex formulated a plan to assassinate Price. The opportunity came when Price arranged a private meeting with Rebecca at a secluded villa outside the city. The villa was a retreat, far from prying eyes and heavily guarded. But Alex was prepared.

On the night of the meeting, Alex made his way to the villa, using the information provided by Rebecca to bypass the security measures. He infiltrated the property with practiced ease, neutralizing the guards with silent precision. Inside, he found Price and Rebecca engaged in conversation, unaware of the danger lurking in the shadows.

Alex moved swiftly, his silenced pistol aimed at Price. He fired a single shot, the bullet finding its mark with lethal accuracy. Price slumped to the floor, her eyes wide with shock and disbelief. Rebecca gasped, her hand covering her mouth as she stared at Alex.

"It's done," Alex said, his voice calm and steady. "Price is dead, and her crimes will be exposed. You need to leave now, Rebecca. Go somewhere safe."

Rebecca nodded, tears streaming down her face. She thanked Alex and fled the villa, disappearing into the night. Alex stayed behind, ensuring that all traces of his presence were erased. He then made his way back to the city, his mission complete.

The assassination of Governor Evelyn Price sent shockwaves through Veridan. The news broke the following morning, dominating the headlines and igniting a firestorm of controversy. The government was thrown into disarray, with officials scrambling to contain the fallout. The Veridan Accord, now in the hands of the media, was published in full, exposing the depth of corruption and collusion between Price and her corporate allies.

Inspector Carr, undeterred by the chaos, intensified his efforts to find the assassin. He knew that the killings of Caldwell, Hawke, and Price were connected, and he was determined to uncover the truth. Carr's investigation led him to Rebecca, who had gone into hiding but was eventually tracked down by the task force.

Under pressure, Rebecca revealed her involvement with Alex and provided details about the villa meeting. Carr used this information to piece together a profile of the assassin, narrowing down potential suspects. He was closing in on Alex, the noose tightening with each passing day.

As the political landscape of Veridan continued to shift, new alliances were formed, and old enemies resurfaced. The public, now aware of the Veridan Accord, demanded sweeping reforms and accountability from their leaders. Protests erupted across the city, with citizens calling for the resignation of corrupt officials and the dismantling of the corporate stranglehold on the government.

In this volatile environment, Alex received a new message from The Handler. The voice was calm and composed, but the words carried a sense of urgency:

"Alex, you've done well. Price's death and the exposure of the Accord have dealt a significant blow to our enemies. But our work is not finished. Your next target is Prime Minister Eleanor Wexler. This will be the most challenging mission yet, but it is essential for our cause. Details to follow."

Prime Minister Eleanor Wexler was the most powerful figure in Veridan, a leader who had navigated the treacherous waters of politics with skill and determination. Taking her down would be a monumental task, requiring every ounce of Alex's training and expertise. But he understood the importance of the mission. Wexler's removal would create a power vacuum, forcing the hidden forces to reveal themselves and allowing The Handler's true plan to unfold.

As he prepared for the next mission, Alex couldn't help but reflect on the path that had brought him to this point. He had become a tool in a larger game, a pawn in the hands of The Handler. But he also understood the necessity of his actions. The corruption and deceit that permeated Veridan's government needed to be exposed, and sometimes, the only way to do that was through drastic measures.

The shadows of power were vast and formidable, but Alex was determined to bring them into the light, no matter the cost. The next phase of his mission would be the most dangerous yet, but he was ready. The battle for Veridan's soul was far from over, and Alex Morgan was prepared to fight until the end.

As the city of Veridan continued to pulse with life and tension, Alex knew that each mission brought him closer to the truth and to the reckoning that awaited in the shadows. The unseen threats that loomed over the city were formidable, but Alex was undeterred. He was a weapon, forged in the fires of betrayal and loss, and he would see his mission through to its conclusion.

The next target was in sight, and the shadows of power trembled in anticipation. Alex Morgan, the political assassin, was ready to strike once more, driven by a desire for justice and retribution. The path he walked was a dangerous one, but it was a path he had chosen willingly, and he would follow it to the end.

Chapter 4: The Governor's Gambit

Veridan was a city in turmoil. The recent assassinations of high-ranking officials had thrown the political landscape into chaos, leaving a power vacuum that threatened to destabilize the entire nation. Amidst this backdrop of uncertainty and fear, Governor Evelyn Price saw an opportunity. Known for her cunning and ruthlessness, Price was determined to exploit the crisis for her own gain. Unbeknownst to her, Alex Morgan, the assassin responsible for the recent killings, had set his sights on her next.

Alex knew that the key to successfully eliminating Price lay in infiltrating her inner circle. Price was a formidable adversary, her security detail nearly impenetrable, and her schedule tightly controlled. To get close enough to execute his mission, Alex needed to become one of the people she trusted.

The first step in his plan was to gather intelligence. Alex began by surveilling Price's known associates, identifying those who were closest to her. Among them was Robert Chambers, Price's chief of staff and confidant. Chambers was a loyalist, fiercely protective of the governor and privy to her most guarded secrets. If Alex could gain Chambers' trust, he would have a direct line to Price.

Alex crafted a new identity for this mission. He became "David Lawson," a political consultant with a reputation for discretion and effectiveness. Using forged credentials and a carefully constructed backstory, Alex approached Chambers, offering his services during this time of crisis. The city was in desperate need of stability, and Price's administration was scrambling to maintain control. Chambers, wary but intrigued by Lawson's credentials, agreed to a meeting.

The meeting took place in a high-end restaurant, a neutral ground where Chambers could assess the newcomer without feeling threatened. Alex played his part flawlessly, presenting himself as a seasoned consultant with valuable insights into crisis management. He spoke of strategies to bolster public confidence, ways to navigate the political fallout, and methods to neutralize opposition. Chambers listened intently, his interest piqued by Alex's proposals.

Over the next few weeks, Alex worked closely with Chambers, ingratiating himself into Price's inner circle. He attended meetings, offered advice, and slowly built a rapport with the key players in Price's administration. His efforts paid off, and soon he was granted access to the governor herself.

Price was every bit as formidable as Alex had expected. She exuded confidence and authority, her presence commanding the room. But Alex noticed something else—a hint of paranoia, a flicker of fear behind her steely gaze. The recent assassinations had shaken her, and she was determined to consolidate her power in the face of growing unrest.

As Alex continued to embed himself within Price's circle, he began to uncover the true extent of her plans. Price was not merely seeking to survive the crisis; she was aiming to exploit it for her own gain. She had identified a series of national vulnerabilities—economic, social, and political—that she intended to leverage to solidify her control.

One of the key components of her plan was the exploitation of a looming economic crisis. Veridan's economy was already under strain, and Price intended to push it to the brink, creating a situation where her intervention would appear necessary and benevolent. She had made secret deals with several powerful corporations, promising them lucrative contracts and policy favors in exchange for their support.

Alex's investigation led him to a clandestine meeting between Price and the CEOs of these corporations. The meeting was held at a secluded estate outside the city, a place where they could discuss their plans without fear of eavesdroppers. Alex, now trusted by Chambers and the inner circle, was able to attend the meeting under the guise of providing strategic advice.

The estate was a fortress, surrounded by high walls and guarded by a private security force. As Alex entered the opulent mansion, he felt the weight of the task ahead. He needed to gather enough evidence to expose Price's conspiracy and eliminate her before she could execute her plans.

The meeting took place in a lavish conference room, with Price at the head of the table. The CEOs, representing some of the most powerful corporations in Veridan, were present, their faces a mix of greed and anticipation. Price outlined her vision: she would engineer a controlled economic collapse, allowing her to step in as a savior. In return, the corporations would receive government contracts, tax breaks, and regulatory leniency.

Alex listened carefully, his mind racing as he recorded the conversation using a concealed device. The evidence he was gathering was damning, enough to bring down Price and her allies if it reached the public. But he also knew that he needed to act quickly. The longer Price remained in power, the more damage she could do.

After the meeting, Alex slipped away to a secluded part of the estate, where he transmitted the recordings to a secure server. He then prepared for the next phase of his plan: the assassination of Governor Evelyn Price. The meeting had provided him with a crucial piece of information—Price's vulnerability. She believed herself untouchable within the confines of her fortified estate, but Alex intended to prove otherwise.

The night of the assassination, Alex made his way back to the estate under the cover of darkness. He used the knowledge he had gained from his time within Price's circle to bypass security measures and navigate the mansion. His target was in her private quarters, a luxurious suite on the top floor.

Alex approached with the stealth and precision that had become his trademark. He neutralized the guards with silent efficiency, using tranquilizer darts to ensure they would not raise the alarm. As he reached the entrance to Price's suite, he paused, his senses heightened by the adrenaline coursing through his veins.

Inside the suite, Price was alone, reviewing documents on her desk. She looked up as Alex entered, a moment of surprise flashing across her face before it was replaced by cold determination.

"Who are you?" she demanded, her hand moving toward a concealed panic button.

Alex moved swiftly, his silenced pistol aimed at Price. "Your time is up, Governor," he said, his voice steady. "This ends tonight."

Price's eyes narrowed, her hand freezing in midair. "You don't know what you're doing. Killing me won't change anything."

"You're wrong," Alex replied. "Your plans end here. The people of Veridan deserve better than to be pawns in your game."

Before Price could respond, Alex pulled the trigger, the shot echoing softly in the room. Price slumped over her desk, a look of shock and defiance frozen on her face. Alex quickly retrieved the documents she had been reviewing, adding them to the evidence he had already gathered.

As he exited the mansion, Alex felt a mix of satisfaction and unease. The mission had been a success, but he couldn't shake the feeling that he was being manipulated. The Handler's motives were becoming increasingly unclear, and Alex began to question the true purpose behind his assignments.

Back at his apartment, Alex reviewed the evidence he had collected. The recordings from the meeting, the documents from Price's suite—it was all damning. He prepared to send the information to The Handler, but he hesitated, a nagging doubt creeping into his mind.

Who was The Handler, really? And what was their endgame? Alex had always operated under the assumption that his missions were part of a larger plan to expose corruption and bring about justice. But the more he uncovered, the more he realized that he was merely a pawn in a game he didn't fully understand.

Despite his reservations, Alex sent the evidence to The Handler, knowing that it was too late to turn back now. The response was swift and cryptic, as always:

"Well done, Alex. Price's death and the exposure of her plans will send a clear message. Your next target will be provided soon. Stay vigilant."

Alex sat back, his mind racing with questions. The Handler's message offered no clarity, only more uncertainty. He knew he couldn't trust anyone, but he also knew that he couldn't stop now. There were still threats to be eliminated, still secrets to be uncovered.

As the city of Veridan continued to grapple with the fallout from Price's assassination, Alex prepared for the next phase of his mission. The shadows of power were vast and formidable, but he was determined to bring them into the light, no matter the cost.

The days following Price's assassination were a whirlwind of activity. The media erupted with the news, speculating on the implications for Veridan's political future. Protests broke out across the city, with citizens demanding accountability and justice. The government, already weakened by the previous assassinations, struggled to maintain control.

Inspector Samuel Carr, undeterred by the chaos, intensified his investigation. He was convinced that the recent string of killings was connected, and he was determined to uncover the truth. Carr's relentless pursuit of the assassin had made him a prominent figure in the media, and his reputation as a tenacious investigator grew with each passing day.

Alex, meanwhile, kept a low profile, watching the events unfold from the safety of his apartment. He knew that Carr was getting closer, and he needed to stay one step ahead. His next target had not yet been revealed, but he was certain that it would be another high-profile figure, someone whose death would further destabilize the already fragile political landscape.

As he waited for instructions from The Handler, Alex continued to gather information. He hacked into government databases, monitored communications, and kept tabs on the key players in Veridan's political arena. The more he uncovered, the clearer it became that the conspiracy he was fighting against was deeper and more insidious than he had initially thought.

One evening, as Alex was reviewing his findings, he received a message from The Handler. The screen flickered to life, displaying a new target: Prime Minister Eleanor Wexler. The message was brief but conveyed a sense of urgency:

"Alex, your next target is Prime Minister Eleanor Wexler. This will be your most challenging mission yet. Wexler's removal is crucial to our cause. Details to follow."

Prime Minister Wexler was the most powerful figure in Veridan, a leader who had managed to maintain her position despite the recent turmoil. Taking her down would be a monumental task, requiring unparalleled precision and planning. But Alex understood the significance of the mission. Wexler's removal would create a power vacuum, forcing the hidden forces to reveal themselves and allowing The Handler's true plan to unfold.

As he began to prepare for the mission, Alex couldn't shake the feeling that he was part of something much larger, a game with stakes higher than he had ever imagined. The path he walked was a dangerous one, but he was committed to seeing it through, driven by a sense of justice and a desire for retribution.

The next few days were spent in intense preparation. Alex conducted thorough reconnaissance on Wexler's movements and schedule, identifying potential vulnerabilities and opportunities. He hacked into security systems, gathered intelligence on her bodyguards, and mapped out the layout of her residence and office.

Wexler was a creature of habit, her routine highly predictable. She attended daily briefings at the Prime Minister's office, held meetings with top advisors, and participated in public events. Her security detail was tight, but Alex knew that even the most fortified defenses had weaknesses.

The breakthrough came when Alex discovered that Wexler had a private residence in a secluded part of the city, a place where she went to unwind and escape the pressures of her position. The residence was less guarded than her official residence and office, providing a potential opportunity to strike.

Alex began to formulate his plan. He would infiltrate the private residence, using the cover of darkness to bypass security measures and neutralize the guards. Once inside, he would eliminate Wexler and retrieve any documents or evidence that could further expose the conspiracy.

The night of the mission arrived, and Alex made his way to Wexler's private residence. He approached from a wooded area behind the property, using the dense foliage to conceal his movements. He scaled the high walls and landed silently in the garden, his senses heightened by the adrenaline coursing through his veins.

The first obstacle was the perimeter alarm system, a sophisticated network of sensors and cameras. Alex used a jammer to disable the sensors temporarily, creating a window of opportunity to slip past undetected. He then made his way to a side entrance, picking the lock with practiced ease.

Inside the residence, Alex navigated the dimly lit corridors, his footsteps silent on the plush carpets. He encountered several guards along the way, dispatching them with a combination of hand-to-hand combat and tranquilizer darts. His movements were fluid and precise, a testament to his training and experience.

Wexler's private quarters were located on the top floor, a luxurious suite that offered a stunning view of the city. Alex approached with caution, his silenced pistol at the ready. He found Wexler alone, reviewing documents on her desk. She looked up as he entered, a moment of surprise flashing across her face before it was replaced by cold determination.

"Who are you?" she demanded, her hand moving toward a concealed panic button.

Alex moved swiftly, his weapon aimed at Wexler. "Your time is up, Prime Minister," he said, his voice steady. "This ends tonight."

Wexler's eyes narrowed, her hand freezing in midair. "You don't know what you're doing. Killing me won't change anything."

"You're wrong," Alex replied. "Your plans end here. The people of Veridan deserve better than to be pawns in your game."

Before Wexler could respond, Alex pulled the trigger, the shot echoing softly in the room. Wexler slumped over her desk, a look of shock and defiance frozen on her face. Alex quickly retrieved the documents she had been reviewing, adding them to the evidence he had already gathered.

As he exited the residence, Alex felt a mix of satisfaction and unease. The mission had been a success, but he couldn't shake the feeling that he was being manipulated. The Handler's motives were becoming increasingly unclear, and Alex began to question the true purpose behind his assignments.

Back at his apartment, Alex reviewed the evidence he had collected. The recordings from the meeting with Price, the documents from Wexler's suite—it was all damning. He prepared to send the information to The Handler, but he hesitated, a nagging doubt creeping into his mind.

Who was The Handler, really? And what was their endgame? Alex had always operated under the assumption that his missions were part of a larger plan to expose corruption and bring about justice. But the more he uncovered, the more he realized that he was merely a pawn in a game he didn't fully understand.

Despite his reservations, Alex sent the evidence to The Handler, knowing that it was too late to turn back now. The response was swift and cryptic, as always:

"Well done, Alex. Wexler's death and the exposure of her plans will send a clear message. Your next target will be provided soon. Stay vigilant."

Alex sat back, his mind racing with questions. The Handler's message offered no clarity, only more uncertainty. He knew he couldn't trust anyone, but he also knew that he couldn't stop now. There were still threats to be eliminated, still secrets to be uncovered.

As the city of Veridan continued to grapple with the fallout from Wexler's assassination, Alex prepared for the next phase of his mission. The shadows of power were vast and formidable, but he was determined to bring them into the light, no matter the cost.

The days following Wexler's assassination were a whirlwind of activity. The media erupted with the news, speculating on the implications for Veridan's political future. Protests broke out across the city, with citizens demanding accountability and justice. The government, already weakened by the previous assassinations, struggled to maintain control.

Inspector Samuel Carr, undeterred by the chaos, intensified his investigation. He was convinced that the recent string of killings was connected, and he was determined to uncover the truth. Carr's relentless pursuit of the assassin had made him a prominent figure in the media, and his reputation as a tenacious investigator grew with each passing day.

Alex, meanwhile, kept a low profile, watching the events unfold from the safety of his apartment. He knew that Carr was getting closer, and he needed to stay one step ahead. His next target had not yet been revealed, but he was certain that it would be another high-profile figure, someone whose death would further destabilize the already fragile political landscape.

As he waited for instructions from The Handler, Alex continued to gather information. He hacked into government databases, monitored communications, and kept tabs on the key players in Veridan's political arena. The more he uncovered, the clearer it became that the conspiracy he was fighting against was deeper and more insidious than he had initially thought.

One evening, as Alex was reviewing his findings, he received a message from The Handler. The screen flickered to life, displaying a new target: Prime Minister Eleanor Wexler. The message was brief but conveyed a sense of urgency:

"Alex, your next target is Prime Minister Eleanor Wexler. This will be your most challenging mission yet. Wexler's removal is crucial to our cause. Details to follow."

Prime Minister Wexler was the most powerful figure in Veridan, a leader who had managed to maintain her position despite the recent turmoil. Taking her down would be a monumental task, requiring unparalleled precision and planning. But Alex understood the significance of the mission. Wexler's removal would create a power vacuum, forcing the hidden forces to reveal themselves and allowing The Handler's true plan to unfold.

As he began to prepare for the mission, Alex couldn't shake the feeling that he was part of something much larger, a game with stakes higher than he had ever imagined. The path he walked was a dangerous one, but he was committed to seeing it through, driven by a sense of justice and a desire for retribution.

The next few days were spent in intense preparation. Alex conducted thorough reconnaissance on Wexler's movements and schedule, identifying potential vulnerabilities and opportunities. He hacked into security systems, gathered intelligence on her bodyguards, and mapped out the layout of her residence and office.

Wexler was a creature of habit, her routine highly predictable. She attended daily briefings at the Prime Minister's office, held meetings with top advisors, and participated in public events. Her security detail was tight, but Alex knew that even the most fortified defenses had weaknesses.

The breakthrough came when Alex discovered that Wexler had a private residence in a secluded part of the city, a place where she went to unwind and escape the pressures of her position. The residence was less guarded than her official residence and office, providing a potential opportunity to strike.

Alex began to formulate his plan. He would infiltrate the private residence, using the cover of darkness to bypass security measures and neutralize the guards. Once inside, he would eliminate Wexler and retrieve any documents or evidence that could further expose the conspiracy.

The night of the mission arrived, and Alex made his way to Wexler's private residence. He approached from a wooded area behind the property, using the dense foliage to conceal his movements. He scaled the high walls and landed silently in the garden, his senses heightened by the adrenaline coursing through his veins.

The first obstacle was the perimeter alarm system, a sophisticated network of sensors and cameras. Alex used a jammer to disable the sensors temporarily, creating a window of opportunity to slip past undetected. He then made his way to a side entrance, picking the lock with practiced ease.

Inside the residence, Alex navigated the dimly lit corridors, his footsteps silent on the plush carpets. He encountered several guards along the way, dispatching them with a combination of hand-to-hand combat and tranquilizer darts. His movements were fluid and precise, a testament to his training and experience.

Wexler's private quarters were located on the top floor, a luxurious suite that offered a stunning view of the city. Alex approached with caution, his silenced pistol at the ready. He found Wexler alone, reviewing documents on her desk. She looked up as he entered, a moment of surprise flashing across her face before it was replaced by cold determination.

"Who are you?" she demanded, her hand moving toward a concealed panic button.

Alex moved swiftly, his weapon aimed at Wexler. "Your time is up, Prime Minister," he said, his voice steady. "This ends tonight."

Wexler's eyes narrowed, her hand freezing in midair. "You don't know what you're doing. Killing me won't change anything."

"You're wrong," Alex replied. "Your plans end here. The people of Veridan deserve better than to be pawns in your game."

Before Wexler could respond, Alex pulled the trigger, the shot echoing softly in the room. Wexler slumped over her desk, a look of shock and defiance frozen on her face. Alex quickly retrieved the documents she had been reviewing, adding them to the evidence he had already gathered.

As he exited the residence, Alex felt a mix of satisfaction and unease. The mission had been a success, but he couldn't shake the feeling that he was being manipulated. The Handler's motives were becoming increasingly unclear, and Alex began to question the true purpose behind his assignments.

Back at his apartment, Alex reviewed the evidence he had collected. The recordings from the meeting with Price, the documents from Wexler's suite—it was all damning. He prepared to send the information to The Handler, but he hesitated, a nagging doubt creeping into his mind.

Who was The Handler, really? And what was their endgame? Alex had always operated under the assumption that his missions were part of a larger plan to expose corruption and bring about justice. But the more he uncovered, the more he realized that he was merely a pawn in a game he didn't fully understand.

Despite his reservations, Alex sent the evidence to The Handler, knowing that it was too late to turn back now. The response was swift and cryptic, as always:

"Well done, Alex. Wexler's death and the exposure of her plans will send a clear message. Your next target will be provided soon. Stay vigilant."

Alex sat back, his mind racing with questions. The Handler's message offered no clarity, only more uncertainty. He knew he couldn't trust anyone, but he also knew that he couldn't stop now. There were still threats to be eliminated, still secrets to be uncovered.

As the city of Veridan continued to grapple with the fallout from Wexler's assassination, Alex prepared for the next phase of his mission. The shadows of power were vast and formidable, but he was determined to bring them into the light, no matter the cost.

Chapter 5: Web of Deceit

The city of Veridan was caught in a storm of political upheaval. The recent string of assassinations had left the government in disarray, and the death of Governor Evelyn Price only added fuel to the fire. In the power vacuum that followed, chaos reigned. Political alliances shifted, new factions emerged, and the streets buzzed with whispers of conspiracy and corruption. It was a city on the brink, teetering between order and anarchy.

Amidst this turmoil, Alex Morgan continued his mission. The successful assassination of Price had provided him with crucial evidence, but it had also raised more questions than it answered. As he reviewed the documents and recordings he had collected, Alex began to see the outlines of a larger scheme, one that extended far beyond the individual targets he had been assigned.

The Veridan Accord, the secret document outlining the alliance between Price and powerful corporations, was the key. It detailed plans for the privatization of public services, the exploitation of natural resources, and the undermining of democratic institutions. But it also hinted at something even more sinister: a coordinated effort to destabilize the government and seize control through a series of orchestrated crises.

As Alex delved deeper into the information, he started to connect the dots. The assassinations were not random acts of violence; they were part of a calculated strategy to remove obstacles and consolidate power. Each target had been carefully chosen to weaken the existing power structure and pave the way for a new regime. The more Alex uncovered, the more he realized that he was entangled in a web of deceit that stretched to the highest levels of power.

One name kept recurring in the documents: Marcus Steele. A charismatic populist leader, Steele had risen to prominence on a platform of reform and justice. He had positioned himself as a champion of the people, railing against corruption and promising to restore integrity to the government. But beneath his polished exterior, Alex suspected a different agenda. Steele's name appeared alongside those of corporate executives and politicians, suggesting that he was deeply involved in the conspiracy.

As Alex prepared to investigate Steele, he became aware of another presence on his trail. Sarah Mitchell, a tenacious investigative journalist, had been following the string of assassinations with keen interest. Known for her relentless pursuit of the truth, Mitchell had a reputation for uncovering hidden scandals and exposing corruption. Her articles on the recent political upheaval had gained significant attention, and she was determined to get to the bottom of the mystery.

Mitchell's investigation led her to the same conclusions that Alex had reached. She saw the connections between the assassinations and the larger conspiracy, and she began to piece together a narrative that threatened to expose the shadowy figures behind the scenes. Her relentless pursuit of the truth put her on a collision course with Alex, as she sought to uncover the identity of the assassin responsible for the killings.

Alex first became aware of Mitchell's interest when he noticed her at a press conference held by Marcus Steele. She was in the front row, her sharp eyes fixed on Steele as he delivered a fiery speech. Her questions were incisive, probing into Steele's connections and challenging his narrative. Alex watched her with a mix of admiration and wariness, recognizing a kindred spirit in her quest for justice.

Over the next few days, Alex kept a close eye on Mitchell's movements. He hacked into her communications, monitored her contacts, and tracked her investigations. He saw that she was closing in on the truth, piecing together the connections between the assassinations and the larger conspiracy. Her determination was both impressive and dangerous, and Alex knew that it was only a matter of time before their paths crossed.

As Alex gathered intelligence on Steele, he saw that the populist leader was preparing for a major rally. The event was set to take place in Veridan's central square, a massive public gathering that would draw thousands of supporters. Steele's speeches had a magnetic effect on his audience, stirring emotions and rallying people to his cause. It was the perfect opportunity for Alex to strike, but it also posed significant risks.

The rally was heavily guarded, with a large security detail and multiple checkpoints. Steele would be surrounded by bodyguards, making it difficult to get close enough for a clean shot. But Alex was undeterred. He began to plan the operation with meticulous detail, identifying potential entry points and exit routes, studying the layout of the square, and analyzing Steele's movements.

The night before the rally, Alex made his way to a vantage point overlooking the square. He set up his equipment, a high-powered sniper rifle with a silencer, and waited. The hours passed slowly, and as dawn approached, the square began to fill with people. Supporters gathered, waving flags and banners, their voices rising in anticipation.

Alex watched through the scope as Steele arrived, stepping onto the stage to a roar of applause. He began his speech, his voice amplified by the sound system, his words resonating with the crowd. Alex adjusted his aim, his finger on the trigger, waiting for the perfect moment.

As he focused on his target, Alex's thoughts drifted to The Handler. The mysterious figure had guided him through each mission, providing information and instructions, but never revealing their true identity or motives. Alex had followed orders without question, driven by a desire for justice and a belief that he was making a difference. But now, with the scope trained on Steele, he began to doubt.

Who was The Handler? What was their ultimate goal? And how did Alex fit into their plans? The questions gnawed at him, eroding his certainty. He had always believed that his actions were part of a larger effort to expose corruption and bring about change, but the more he uncovered, the more he realized that he was a pawn in a game he didn't fully understand.

As Steele's speech reached a crescendo, Alex steadied his aim, ready to pull the trigger. But in that moment, a new thought emerged. What if Steele was not the true enemy? What if his death would only further the agenda of those who sought to control Veridan from the shadows?

Alex lowered the rifle, his mind racing. He couldn't shake the feeling that he was being manipulated, that the true architects of the conspiracy remained hidden. He needed answers, and he knew that the only way to get them was to confront The Handler directly.

Abandoning his position, Alex made his way back to his apartment, his thoughts a whirlwind of conflicting emotions. He had always been a soldier, following orders without question, but now he found himself questioning everything. The mission, the targets, the motives—it all seemed shrouded in deception.

As he prepared to contact The Handler, Alex received an unexpected visitor. Sarah Mitchell had tracked him down, her investigative skills and determination leading her to his doorstep. She confronted him, her eyes blazing with a mixture of anger and curiosity.

"Who are you?" she demanded. "And why are you killing these people?"

Alex regarded her calmly, recognizing the intensity of her pursuit. "I'm trying to expose the corruption that threatens this city," he replied. "But it's more complicated than you think."

Mitchell's gaze didn't waver. "I've seen the connections. I know there's a larger conspiracy at play. But I need to understand why you're involved. Who are you working for?"

Alex hesitated, weighing his options. He saw in Mitchell a potential ally, someone who shared his desire for justice, but he also knew the risks of revealing too much. After a moment, he decided to take a chance.

"I'm working for someone known only as The Handler," he said. "They provide the targets, the information, the resources. But I'm starting to question their true motives."

Mitchell's expression softened slightly. "I want to help. But I need to know everything. No more secrets."

Alex nodded, realizing that he needed her help as much as she needed his. "Agreed. But first, we need to find out who The Handler really is. And why they're orchestrating these assassinations."

The two of them spent the next few hours sharing information, piecing together the web of deceit that had ensnared Veridan. Mitchell revealed her findings on Steele, showing how his populist rhetoric masked his deeper connections to the conspiracy. Alex shared his insights into the Veridan Accord and the hidden alliances that fueled the corruption.

Together, they formulated a plan. They would use the rally as a cover to gather more intelligence on Steele and his allies. Alex would attend the event as a bodyguard, using his skills to blend in and protect Steele while keeping a close watch on his movements. Mitchell would work from the sidelines, using her press credentials to gain access and gather information.

The day of the rally arrived, and Alex took up his position near the stage. He wore the uniform of a security guard, his demeanor calm and professional.

Mitchell mingled with the crowd, her camera and notebook in hand, ready to capture any incriminating evidence.

As Steele began his speech, Alex scanned the crowd, looking for any signs of danger. He saw Mitchell in the front row, her eyes fixed on Steele, her expression intense. The crowd was a sea of faces, their emotions a mix of hope and anger, their voices rising in response to Steele's words.

Suddenly, Alex noticed a group of men moving through the crowd, their movements coordinated and purposeful. He recognized them as operatives, likely working for the same shadowy figures behind the conspiracy. They were making their way toward the stage, their intentions clear.

Alex moved swiftly, intercepting the men before they could reach Steele. He engaged them in a fierce struggle, his training and experience giving him the upper hand. The fight was brutal but brief, and Alex emerged victorious, leaving the men incapacitated and unable to carry out their mission.

As the rally continued, Alex and Mitchell regrouped, their bond strengthened by the shared danger and their mutual quest for the truth. They had thwarted the immediate threat, but they knew that the true battle lay ahead. The conspiracy was vast and powerful, and they were only beginning to unravel its depths.

That evening, back at Alex's apartment, they reviewed the evidence they had gathered. Mitchell's photographs and notes provided valuable insights into Steele's connections and the operatives' intentions. Alex's instincts had been correct: Steele was a pawn in the larger game, his populist rhetoric masking a more sinister agenda.

As they prepared to confront The Handler, Alex received a new message. The screen flickered to life, displaying a series of coordinates and a brief instruction:

"Meet at the designated location. It's time to learn the truth."

Alex and Mitchell exchanged a determined look. They were on the brink of discovering the true architects of the conspiracy, but they also knew the risks. The journey ahead would be fraught with danger, but they were ready to face it together.

The coordinates led them to an abandoned warehouse on the outskirts of the city, a place shrouded in darkness and secrecy. Alex and Mitchell approached cautiously, their senses heightened by the anticipation of what lay ahead. They entered the warehouse, their footsteps echoing in the vast, empty space.

A figure emerged from the shadows, their face obscured by a hood. The voice was familiar, calm and composed, the same voice that had guided Alex through each mission.

"Welcome, Alex. And welcome, Ms. Mitchell. I see you've found each other. Good. It's time you both understood the bigger picture."

Alex's eyes narrowed. "Who are you? And what is your true goal?"

The figure stepped forward, revealing a face that Alex recognized but had never expected. It was someone he had trusted, someone who had been a part of his life before the assassinations began.

"I'm someone who shares your desire for justice," the figure said. "But our methods differ. I've orchestrated these events to expose the corruption and bring about change. But there's more at stake than you realize."

As the figure began to explain, Alex and Mitchell listened intently, their understanding deepening with each word. They learned about the true extent of the conspiracy, the hidden forces manipulating Veridan from the shadows, and the ultimate goal: a complete overhaul of the existing power structure.

The journey ahead would be perilous, but Alex and Mitchell were ready. They had uncovered the web of deceit that threatened their city, and they were determined to bring the truth to light. Together, they would face the unseen threats, confront the shadowy figures, and fight for a future free from corruption and control.

As they prepared to embark on the next phase of their mission, Alex felt a renewed sense of purpose. The path was fraught with danger, but he was no longer alone. With Mitchell by his side, he was ready to challenge the shadows of power and expose the web of deceit that had ensnared Veridan.

The battle for the city's soul had only just begun, and Alex Morgan was prepared to fight until the end.

Chapter 6: A Dangerous Game

The atmosphere in Veridan grew more tense by the day. The assassinations had left a trail of confusion and fear, causing the government to tighten security measures across the board. Nowhere was this more evident than around Marcus Steele, the charismatic populist leader whose influence seemed to grow with each passing day. Steele's security detail was now impenetrable, with guards at every corner and surveillance at every turn.

Alex Morgan, ever the master strategist, knew he had to devise an elaborate plan to eliminate Steele. The stakes had never been higher, and failure was not an option. As he observed Steele's movements from the shadows, Alex noticed the increased vigilance of his security team. They were thorough, professional, and uncompromising. It would take more than just skill and precision to breach their defenses.

Meanwhile, Sarah Mitchell was deep in her own investigation. The evidence she had gathered pointed to a complex web of deceit involving high-ranking officials and powerful corporations. As she connected the dots, she began to uncover clues linking the assassinations to a secretive organization known as The Syndicate. This shadowy group operated behind the scenes, pulling strings and manipulating events to their advantage.

Sarah's relentless pursuit of the truth brought her closer to the heart of the conspiracy. She pored over documents, conducted interviews, and followed leads that took her to the darkest corners of Veridan. Her determination to expose The Syndicate became a driving force, pushing her beyond her limits. She knew that revealing their existence would be a game-changer, but she also understood the dangers involved. The closer she got to the truth, the more she put herself in the crosshairs of powerful enemies.

As Alex planned the assassination, he remained in close contact with Sarah. Their partnership had become essential, each providing the other with crucial insights and support. They knew that Steele's death would send shockwaves through the nation, but it was a necessary step in their quest to dismantle The Syndicate's grip on Veridan.

The opportunity to eliminate Steele presented itself in the form of a public rally, an event that would draw thousands of supporters and media attention. It was a high-risk scenario, but it also provided the perfect cover for an assassination. Alex began to devise an elaborate plan, one that would require precision, timing, and a bit of luck.

Alex's plan revolved around creating a diversion that would draw Steele's security detail away from him momentarily. He needed to find a way to infiltrate the rally, get close enough to Steele, and execute the hit without getting caught. It was a delicate balance, and any misstep could be fatal.

On the day of the rally, Veridan's central square was a hive of activity. Supporters gathered in droves, waving banners and chanting slogans. The atmosphere was charged with energy and anticipation. Steele's speeches had a magnetic effect on the crowd, his words resonating with those who felt disenfranchised and ignored by the political elite.

Alex moved through the crowd with practiced ease, blending in with the throngs of people. He wore a disguise that made him look like an ordinary supporter, complete with a cap and sunglasses. His eyes constantly scanned the area, noting the positions of the security guards and identifying potential escape routes. He had already scoped out the stage and its surroundings, calculating the best angles for a clean shot.

Meanwhile, Sarah worked behind the scenes, using her press credentials to gain access to restricted areas. She had a dual purpose: to gather evidence and to provide support for Alex. Her investigative instincts had led her to uncover critical information about Steele's connections to The Syndicate. She had documented meetings, recorded conversations, and collected enough evidence to expose Steele's true nature.

As the rally began, Steele took the stage to thunderous applause. His voice boomed through the speakers, his rhetoric igniting the passions of the crowd. Alex watched from a distance, his heart pounding with anticipation. He knew that the window of opportunity would be brief, and he had to be ready.

Alex's diversion involved a carefully orchestrated sequence of events. He had planted a small explosive device in a trash can near the edge of the square, far enough from the stage to avoid casualties but close enough to cause a commotion. The device was set to go off midway through Steele's speech, creating a distraction that would momentarily pull the security detail's attention away from the stage.

As Steele reached a crescendo in his speech, the device detonated with a loud bang. The crowd erupted in confusion and panic, people scattering in all directions. The security guards immediately moved to contain the situation, their focus shifting to the source of the explosion. Alex seized the moment, moving quickly and silently toward the stage.

With the guards distracted, Alex slipped past the barricades and made his way to the back of the stage. He had timed his approach perfectly, using the chaos to his advantage. As he neared the steps leading up to the platform, he pulled out a small, silenced pistol from his jacket. His hand was steady, his mind focused on the task at hand.

Steele, unaware of the imminent danger, continued to address the crowd, trying to calm the panic. His voice was firm, his presence commanding. But as Alex took aim, everything seemed to slow down. The noise of the crowd faded, the chaos became a distant blur, and all that mattered was the target in his sights.

With a deep breath, Alex squeezed the trigger. The shot was precise, the bullet finding its mark with lethal accuracy. Steele's voice faltered, his body stiffened, and he crumpled to the ground. For a moment, there was silence, a stunned disbelief that swept through the crowd. Then, pandemonium erupted.

Alex moved swiftly, using the confusion to make his escape. He blended back into the crowd, his disguise helping him disappear into the throngs of panicked people. He had planned his exit meticulously, and within minutes, he was clear of the square, making his way to a safe house on the outskirts of the city.

Sarah, who had been documenting the rally from a vantage point, captured the entire sequence on her camera. She had anticipated the diversion and positioned herself strategically to document both the explosion and the aftermath. As soon as she saw Steele go down, she knew Alex had succeeded. She quickly gathered her equipment and slipped away, heading to a secure location where she could review the footage and continue her investigation.

The assassination of Marcus Steele sent shockwaves through Veridan. The news spread like wildfire, dominating headlines and social media. The nation was in a state of shock, grappling with the sudden and violent removal of a prominent political figure. Conspiracy theories flourished, and the government responded with a heavy-handed crackdown on dissent.

Inspector Samuel Carr, who had been investigating the string of assassinations, was now more determined than ever to find the assassin. Steele's death added a new urgency to his mission, and he vowed to leave no stone unturned. He intensified his efforts, coordinating with other agencies and expanding the scope of the investigation.

Meanwhile, Sarah worked tirelessly to connect the pieces of the puzzle. Her investigation into The Syndicate had uncovered a vast network of influence and corruption, stretching across multiple sectors of society. She knew that exposing them would be a monumental task, but she was committed to revealing the truth.

As she reviewed the footage from the rally, Sarah noticed something that made her heart race. In the chaos following the explosion, she had captured a brief glimpse of Alex's face. It was a fleeting moment, but it confirmed her suspicions about his involvement. She knew she had to find him and convince him to work with her.

Using her contacts, Sarah managed to track down Alex's location. She approached him cautiously, knowing that trust was a fragile thing. When they met, she showed him the footage, her eyes searching his for a reaction.

"You did it," she said quietly. "You took out Steele. But we both know this is just the beginning. We need to expose The Syndicate. We need to bring them down."

Alex nodded, his expression serious. "I know. But it's not going to be easy. They're powerful, and they have eyes everywhere. We need to be careful."

Sarah agreed, her resolve unwavering. "I have evidence, documents, recordings. We can use it to build a case, to show the world what's really happening. But I need your help. We need to work together."

Alex considered her words, weighing the risks and the potential rewards. He knew that Sarah was right. The Syndicate was a formidable enemy, and exposing them would require a combined effort. He reached out his hand, a gesture of solidarity.

"Alright," he said. "Let's do this. Together."

Over the next few days, Alex and Sarah worked in tandem, pooling their resources and sharing information. They created a plan to expose The

Syndicate, using the evidence they had gathered to build a comprehensive case. Sarah's investigative skills and media connections proved invaluable, while Alex's strategic mind and operational expertise provided the necessary edge.

As they delved deeper into The Syndicate's operations, they uncovered more layers of corruption and deceit. They identified key players, traced financial transactions, and documented meetings. The web of deceit was vast, but they were determined to unravel it.

Their efforts culminated in a daring operation to intercept a high-level meeting of The Syndicate's leaders. The meeting was set to take place in a remote location, far from the prying eyes of the public. Alex and Sarah knew that this was their chance to gather irrefutable evidence and expose the organization once and for all.

On the night of the meeting, Alex and Sarah made their way to the location, their hearts pounding with anticipation. They had enlisted the help of a few trusted allies, individuals who shared their commitment to justice and were willing to take risks for the greater good.

As they approached the meeting site, Alex deployed a series of surveillance devices, capturing audio and video of the proceedings. They watched from a distance as The Syndicate's leaders gathered, their conversation revealing the full extent of their plans. The leaders discussed their strategies, their influence over key political figures, and their intentions to manipulate events for their own gain.

Sarah recorded every word, her camera capturing the faces of those involved. She knew that this evidence would be the key to bringing down The Syndicate. But as they continued to monitor the meeting, they realized that they were not alone.

The Syndicate had anticipated the possibility of surveillance, and they had set a trap. As the meeting concluded, armed operatives emerged from the shadows, surrounding Alex and Sarah's position. The tension was palpable, and Alex knew that they were in a precarious situation.

Thinking quickly, Alex signaled to Sarah and their allies to fall back. They retreated into the darkness, using their knowledge of the terrain to evade their pursuers. The chase was intense, but they managed to outmaneuver their enemies, escaping with the crucial evidence intact.

Back at their safe house, Alex and Sarah reviewed the footage, their faces lit by the glow of the screens. They had captured enough to expose The Syndicate, but they knew that releasing the information would be dangerous. The organization would stop at nothing to protect their interests, and retaliation was inevitable.

Despite the risks, they decided to move forward. They contacted trusted media outlets, providing them with the evidence and coordinating a simultaneous release. The story broke, sending shockwaves through Veridan and beyond. The public was stunned by the revelations, and calls for accountability grew louder.

The government, now under immense pressure, launched an official investigation into The Syndicate. Key figures were arrested, and their assets were seized. The leaders of the conspiracy were exposed, their influence dismantled. The nation began to heal, the shadows of corruption giving way to a renewed sense of hope and justice.

As Veridan slowly regained its footing, Alex and Sarah reflected on their journey. They had faced incredible odds, but their determination and partnership had prevailed. They knew that their work was far from over, but they were ready to face whatever challenges lay ahead.

In the end, the successful assassination of Marcus Steele had been a turning point, a catalyst for change. It had shocked the nation and exposed the depths of The Syndicate's corruption. But it had also brought Alex and Sarah together, forging a bond that would continue to drive their pursuit of justice.

As they looked out over the city, Alex and Sarah felt a renewed sense of purpose. They had played a dangerous game, but they had emerged victorious. And they knew that as long as there were shadows to be uncovered and secrets to be revealed, they would continue to fight for a better future.

The battle against The Syndicate was won, but the war for Veridan's soul was far from over. Alex and Sarah stood ready, their resolve unshaken, their mission clear. Together, they would face whatever dangers came their way, knowing that the pursuit of justice was a journey that never truly ended.

Chapter 7: The Puppet Masters

The atmosphere in Veridan was charged with tension. The recent political assassinations had thrown the city into turmoil, and the power vacuum left behind was rapidly being filled by ambitious politicians and shadowy figures. Amidst this chaos, Alex Morgan continued his mission, delving deeper into the murky waters of Veridan's political underbelly. The name "The Syndicate" had surfaced repeatedly during his investigations, and it was clear that this clandestine group was orchestrating the events that were shaking the city to its core.

As Alex gathered more information, he began to see the outlines of The Syndicate's operations. They were a secretive organization with connections to powerful corporations, politicians, and military leaders. Their influence extended far and wide, manipulating political events to serve their interests. The Syndicate's ultimate goal was to control Veridan by placing their puppets in key positions of power, ensuring that their agenda would be implemented without opposition.

Despite his best efforts, Alex found it difficult to uncover the true identity and motives of The Handler, the enigmatic figure who had been guiding him through his missions. The Handler's messages were always brief and cryptic, providing just enough information to complete the assignments but never revealing their true intentions. Alex couldn't shake the feeling that he was being used as a pawn in a much larger game, but he had no choice but to continue his work.

Meanwhile, Sarah Mitchell's investigation was bringing her dangerously close to the truth. Her relentless pursuit of justice had led her to uncover critical information about The Syndicate's operations, and she was determined to expose their machinations. Sarah's articles had gained significant attention, and her reputation as a fearless journalist grew with each revelation. However, her work had also attracted the attention of The Syndicate, putting her life at risk.

One evening, as Alex reviewed the intelligence he had gathered, he received a new message from The Handler. The screen flickered to life, displaying the name of his next target: General Victor Blackwood, the head of The Syndicate's security. The message was brief but conveyed a sense of urgency:

"Alex, your next target is General Victor Blackwood. He is a key figure in The Syndicate's operations, responsible for their security and enforcement. Eliminating him will weaken their control and expose their vulnerabilities. Details to follow."

General Blackwood was a formidable adversary. A former military leader with a reputation for ruthlessness, he had been instrumental in establishing The Syndicate's security apparatus. His network of operatives and informants ensured that The Syndicate's activities remained hidden from public view. Taking him down would be a significant blow to the organization, but it would also be incredibly dangerous.

Alex began to formulate a plan to eliminate Blackwood. He knew that the general was heavily guarded, with multiple layers of security protecting him at all times. The first step was to gather as much information as possible about Blackwood's movements and routines. Alex hacked into government databases, monitored communications, and used his network of contacts to piece together a comprehensive profile of his target.

As he delved deeper into Blackwood's background, Alex uncovered a series of clandestine meetings and financial transactions that linked the general to The Syndicate's most powerful figures. These meetings took place in secure locations, far from prying eyes, and involved the exchange of large sums of money and sensitive information. It was clear that Blackwood was not just a security chief; he was a central figure in The Syndicate's operations.

Sarah, meanwhile, was making significant progress in her investigation. She had uncovered a trail of evidence that pointed to The Syndicate's involvement in the recent assassinations and their efforts to manipulate political events. Her sources provided her with critical information about the organization's inner workings, and she began to piece together a narrative that threatened to expose The Syndicate's true nature.

However, Sarah's work had not gone unnoticed. The Syndicate was aware of her investigation, and they were taking steps to silence her. She received anonymous threats, her sources were intimidated, and her communications were monitored. Despite the danger, Sarah refused to back down. She knew that the truth had to be revealed, no matter the cost.

As Alex and Sarah continued their respective missions, they found themselves working more closely together. Their partnership had become essential, each providing the other with crucial insights and support. They shared information, coordinated their efforts, and protected each other from the ever-present threats posed by The Syndicate.

The breakthrough in their investigation came when Sarah uncovered a key piece of evidence: a list of names and addresses associated with The Syndicate's leadership. This list included politicians, corporate executives, and military leaders, all of whom were complicit in the organization's activities. Among the names was General Victor Blackwood, along with details of his security arrangements and upcoming movements.

Using this information, Alex devised an elaborate plan to eliminate Blackwood. He knew that the general's next meeting with The Syndicate's leaders would take place at a secure compound on the outskirts of the city. The compound was heavily fortified, with multiple layers of security, but it also provided an opportunity for Alex to strike.

The plan involved creating a diversion to draw Blackwood's security detail away from him momentarily. Alex would then infiltrate the compound, get close to Blackwood, and execute the hit. It was a high-risk operation, but Alex was confident in his abilities and the meticulous planning he had undertaken.

On the night of the operation, Alex made his way to the compound, using the cover of darkness to approach undetected. He deployed a series of small explosive devices around the perimeter, set to detonate simultaneously and create a distraction. As the explosions rocked the compound, the security guards scrambled to respond, leaving Blackwood vulnerable.

Alex moved swiftly, using his knowledge of the compound's layout to navigate the corridors and avoid detection. He encountered several guards along the way, dispatching them with silent precision. His heart pounded with anticipation as he neared Blackwood's location.

In the heart of the compound, Blackwood was in a meeting with several high-ranking members of The Syndicate. The explosions had thrown the meeting into chaos, and the leaders were frantically trying to assess the situation. Alex took advantage of the confusion, slipping into the room and positioning himself behind Blackwood.

With a single, swift motion, Alex drew his silenced pistol and fired. The shot was precise, the bullet finding its mark with lethal accuracy. Blackwood slumped over the table, his eyes wide with shock and disbelief. The Syndicate leaders reacted with a mix of fear and anger, but Alex was already on the move, making his escape before they could react.

As Alex exited the compound, he felt a mix of satisfaction and unease. The mission had been a success, but the true battle was just beginning. Blackwood's death would send shockwaves through The Syndicate, but it would also provoke a fierce response. The organization would stop at nothing to protect their interests and eliminate the threat posed by Alex and Sarah.

Back at their safe house, Alex and Sarah reviewed the evidence they had gathered. The list of names and addresses provided a roadmap for their next steps, but it also revealed the full extent of The Syndicate's reach. The organization had infiltrated every level of government and society, and dismantling their operations would require a sustained and coordinated effort.

Sarah's investigation continued to yield valuable insights. She uncovered more details about The Syndicate's activities, including their financial transactions, political connections, and plans for future operations. Her determination to expose the truth drove her to work tirelessly, despite the constant threats to her safety.

As they prepared for the next phase of their mission, Alex and Sarah knew that the road ahead would be perilous. The Syndicate was a formidable enemy, and their reach extended far and wide. But they also knew that they had the tools and the resolve to bring the organization to its knees.

The next target on their list was a high-ranking politician with close ties to The Syndicate. This individual had played a key role in facilitating the organization's activities, using their influence to manipulate events and protect The Syndicate's interests. Taking them down would be a significant step in dismantling the organization, but it would also draw even more attention to Alex and Sarah's efforts.

As they planned their next move, Alex couldn't shake the feeling that The Handler was still watching, still pulling the strings from behind the scenes. The true identity and motives of The Handler remained shrouded in mystery, and Alex knew that uncovering the truth would be crucial to their mission.

Sarah, too, was determined to find out who The Handler really was. Her investigation had brought her closer to the heart of the conspiracy, but she knew that there were still many unanswered questions. Together, she and Alex vowed to uncover the truth, no matter the cost.

As they prepared for their next mission, Alex and Sarah felt a renewed sense of purpose. The battle against The Syndicate was far from over, but they were ready to face whatever challenges lay ahead. They knew that the path they had chosen was fraught with danger, but they were committed to seeing it through to the end.

The successful assassination of General Victor Blackwood had sent a clear message: The Syndicate was not invincible, and their grip on Veridan was beginning to slip. As the city continued to grapple with the fallout from the recent events, Alex and Sarah remained focused on their mission. They were determined to expose the puppet masters who had been manipulating political events and bring them to justice.

The next phase of their mission would be the most challenging yet, but Alex and Sarah were ready. They had faced incredible odds and emerged victorious, and they knew that the battle for Veridan's soul was far from over. Together, they would continue to fight for justice, exposing the shadows of power and dismantling the web of deceit that had ensnared their city.

As they looked out over the city, Alex and Sarah felt a renewed sense of purpose. They had played a dangerous game, but they had emerged stronger and more determined than ever. And they knew that as long as there were puppet masters pulling the strings, they would continue to fight for a future free from corruption and control. The battle was far from over, but they were ready to face whatever dangers came their way, knowing that the pursuit of justice was a journey that never truly ended.

The days following Blackwood's assassination were marked by heightened tension and increased security measures across Veridan. The Syndicate, reeling from the loss of one of their key operatives, responded with a crackdown on suspected threats and a tightening of their internal security. Alex and Sarah had anticipated this reaction and took extra precautions to avoid detection.

Their next target, the high-ranking politician with close ties to The Syndicate, was someone who wielded significant influence in Veridan's government. This individual had been instrumental in passing legislation that benefited The Syndicate's corporate backers and had used their position to shield the organization from scrutiny. Alex and Sarah knew that taking down this politician would deal a significant blow to The Syndicate's operations.

As they gathered intelligence on their new target, Alex and Sarah continued to work closely together, sharing information and coordinating their efforts. They were acutely aware of the dangers they faced, but their resolve was unwavering. They had come too far to turn back now, and they were determined to see their mission through to the end.

Sarah's investigation had uncovered more details about The Syndicate's structure and operations. She had identified several key figures within the organization, including financiers, strategists, and enforcers. This information provided valuable insights into The Syndicate's inner workings and helped Alex and Sarah plan their next moves.

One evening, as they reviewed their findings, Sarah received a tip from one of her trusted sources. The tip indicated that The Syndicate's leadership would be holding a secret meeting to discuss their next steps in response to Blackwood's assassination. The meeting was set to take place at a secure location in the heart of the city, and the source provided the time and address.

Alex and Sarah knew that this was a rare opportunity to gather intelligence and possibly eliminate multiple high-ranking members of The Syndicate in one fell swoop. They began to formulate a plan to infiltrate the meeting and record the proceedings, with the goal of using the evidence to expose the organization's activities.

The location of the meeting was a luxurious penthouse in one of Veridan's most exclusive neighborhoods. The building had state-of-the-art security, including biometric access controls, surveillance cameras, and armed guards. Alex and Sarah knew that gaining access would be challenging, but they were determined to succeed.

On the night of the meeting, Alex and Sarah arrived at the building, using disguises to blend in with the other residents and visitors. Alex had obtained a stolen access card from a contact, which allowed them to bypass the initial security checkpoint. They took the elevator to the top floor, their hearts pounding with anticipation.

As they approached the penthouse, Alex used a device to hack into the building's security system, temporarily disabling the cameras and alarms. They moved quickly and silently, reaching the door to the penthouse without being detected. Alex picked the lock with practiced ease, and they slipped inside.

The penthouse was lavishly decorated, with floor-to-ceiling windows offering stunning views of the city. In the center of the living room, a group of well-dressed individuals sat around a large table, deep in discussion. Alex and Sarah recognized several of them as key figures within The Syndicate, including their current target, the high-ranking politician.

Alex set up a small camera to record the meeting, positioning it discreetly behind a decorative sculpture. He and Sarah then took up positions where they could listen and observe without being seen. The leaders of The Syndicate were discussing their plans in response to the recent events, including strategies to protect their interests and counter the actions of Alex and Sarah.

The conversation revealed the full extent of The Syndicate's influence and their willingness to use any means necessary to achieve their goals. They discussed bribing officials, manipulating media coverage, and even resorting to violence to maintain control. It was clear that The Syndicate was a formidable and ruthless organization, willing to go to any lengths to protect their power.

As the meeting continued, Alex and Sarah's presence was suddenly detected. One of the security guards had noticed the disabled cameras and raised the alarm. The leaders of The Syndicate reacted quickly, ordering their guards to secure the penthouse and find the intruders.

Alex and Sarah knew they had to act fast. They retrieved the camera and made their way to the nearest exit, but they were confronted by armed guards. A fierce firefight ensued, with Alex and Sarah using their training and skills to fight their way out. Bullets flew, and the sounds of gunfire echoed through the penthouse.

Despite the overwhelming odds, Alex and Sarah managed to escape, but not without injuries. They made their way to a safe house, where they treated their wounds and reviewed the footage they had captured. The evidence was damning, providing clear proof of The Syndicate's activities and their plans to manipulate political events.

With the footage in hand, Alex and Sarah contacted their allies in the media and law enforcement, arranging for a coordinated release of the information. The story broke the next day, sending shockwaves through Veridan and beyond. The public was outraged by the revelations, and calls for accountability grew louder.

The government launched a comprehensive investigation into The Syndicate, resulting in the arrest of several key figures and the seizure of their assets. The organization's influence began to wane, and their grip on Veridan weakened. The successful operation had dealt a significant blow to The Syndicate, but Alex and Sarah knew that their work was far from over.

As the city continued to grapple with the fallout from the revelations, Alex and Sarah remained focused on their mission. They had exposed the puppet masters who had been manipulating political events, but they knew that there were still threats to be eliminated and secrets to be uncovered.

The battle against The Syndicate was not yet won, but Alex and Sarah were ready to face whatever challenges lay ahead. Their resolve was stronger than ever, and they were determined to continue fighting for justice and a future free from corruption and control. As they looked out over the city, they felt a renewed sense of purpose, knowing that the pursuit of justice was a journey that never truly ended.

Chapter 8: The General's Fall

The city of Veridan was still reeling from the revelations about The Syndicate. The arrest of several key figures had sent shockwaves through the political landscape, and the public was clamoring for more answers and accountability. Amidst this turmoil, Alex Morgan and Sarah Mitchell knew that their work was far from finished. They had struck a significant blow against The Syndicate, but the organization was still a formidable adversary, and their ultimate plan remained a mystery.

General Victor Blackwood, the head of The Syndicate's security, was their next target. Blackwood was a key figure in the organization, responsible for their enforcement and protection. Taking him down would further weaken The Syndicate and provide Alex and Sarah with the opportunity to uncover their ultimate plan. However, Blackwood's heavily fortified compound posed a significant challenge. It was a fortress, with multiple layers of security and a contingent of loyal guards.

Alex began to formulate a plan to infiltrate the compound and eliminate Blackwood. He conducted thorough reconnaissance, studying the layout of the compound, the security measures in place, and the routines of the guards. Every detail was meticulously analyzed and incorporated into his strategy. He knew that this mission would require precision, timing, and a bit of luck.

Sarah, meanwhile, continued her investigation into The Syndicate. She had gained significant attention for her work, and her reputation as a fearless journalist grew with each revelation. Her articles had put her in the spotlight, but they had also attracted the attention of The Syndicate, making her a target. Despite the danger, Sarah remained committed to exposing the truth.

One evening, as Alex reviewed his plan, Sarah received a message from an unexpected source. It was from Senator Emily Carter, a high-ranking government official known for her integrity and dedication to justice. Senator Carter had been following Sarah's investigation and was impressed by her determination and bravery. She offered her assistance, providing Sarah with access to confidential information and resources that could help in their mission.

Sarah met with Senator Carter in a discreet location, where they discussed The Syndicate's activities and the evidence Sarah had gathered. Carter revealed that she had been investigating The Syndicate for years but had faced significant obstacles and threats. She believed that Sarah's work could be the key to finally bringing the organization to justice. The two women formed a vital alliance, combining their resources and efforts to dismantle The Syndicate.

With Senator Carter's support, Sarah was able to obtain critical information about Blackwood's compound and the security measures in place. This information proved invaluable to Alex as he finalized his plan. The mission was set to take place the following night, under the cover of darkness.

On the night of the operation, Alex made his way to Blackwood's compound, using the knowledge he had gained from his reconnaissance and the information provided by Senator Carter. He approached the compound from a wooded area, using the dense foliage to conceal his movements. The first obstacle was the perimeter fence, equipped with motion sensors and surveillance cameras. Alex used a jammer to disable the sensors temporarily, creating a window of opportunity to slip past undetected.

Once inside the compound, Alex navigated the corridors and courtyards with the stealth of a predator. He encountered several guards along the way, dispatching them with silent precision. His silenced pistol and combat skills ensured that he moved swiftly and efficiently, avoiding detection.

As he approached the main building, Alex encountered a more heavily guarded area. He used a combination of distraction techniques and hand-to-hand combat to neutralize the guards, making his way to Blackwood's private quarters. The tension was palpable as he neared his target, his heart pounding with anticipation.

Inside the quarters, Blackwood was reviewing documents at his desk, unaware of the imminent danger. Alex moved silently, positioning himself behind the general. He drew his silenced pistol, ready to execute the mission. But as he aimed, Blackwood suddenly turned, sensing the presence of an intruder.

A high-stakes confrontation ensued, with Blackwood reaching for his weapon. The two men engaged in a fierce struggle, their movements swift and deadly. Blackwood was a formidable opponent, his military training evident in his combat skills. But Alex's experience and determination gave him the edge.

The fight was brutal and intense, but Alex's precision and skill ultimately prevailed. With a final, decisive move, he incapacitated Blackwood, disarming him and rendering him defenseless. Alex aimed his pistol at the fallen general, his voice steady.

"This ends now, Blackwood. The Syndicate's reign of terror is over."

Blackwood's eyes narrowed, a mix of anger and defiance in his gaze. "You think killing me will stop The Syndicate? You're just a pawn in a game you don't understand."

Alex pulled the trigger, the shot echoing softly in the room. Blackwood slumped over, his life extinguished. Alex quickly searched the quarters, looking for any documents or evidence that could reveal The Syndicate's ultimate plan.

In a hidden compartment behind Blackwood's desk, Alex discovered a trove of documents, maps, and digital files. The information was extensive, detailing The Syndicate's operations, financial transactions, and future plans. Among the documents was a comprehensive plan outlining their ultimate goal: a coordinated effort to destabilize Veridan's government and seize control through a series of orchestrated crises.

Alex knew that this information was crucial to dismantling The Syndicate. He gathered the documents and made his way out of the compound, using the same route he had taken to enter. The guards were still recovering from the initial confrontation, allowing Alex to slip away undetected.

Back at the safe house, Alex and Sarah reviewed the documents, their faces lit by the glow of the computer screens. The evidence was damning, providing a clear picture of The Syndicate's activities and their plans to manipulate political events. The information was enough to bring down the organization, but they needed to ensure that it reached the right people.

With Senator Carter's help, they coordinated a plan to release the information to the public and law enforcement simultaneously. They prepared a comprehensive report, detailing The Syndicate's operations and providing the evidence needed to launch a full-scale investigation. The report was sent to trusted media outlets and government officials, ensuring that the information would be widely disseminated and acted upon.

The following day, the story broke, sending shockwaves through Veridan. The public was outraged by the revelations, and calls for accountability grew louder. The government responded by launching a comprehensive investigation into The Syndicate, resulting in the arrest of several key figures and the seizure of their assets. The organization's influence began to wane, and their grip on Veridan weakened.

As the city continued to grapple with the fallout from the revelations, Alex and Sarah remained focused on their mission. They had exposed the puppet masters who had been manipulating political events, but they knew that there were still threats to be eliminated and secrets to be uncovered.

The successful operation against Blackwood had dealt a significant blow to The Syndicate, but Alex and Sarah knew that their work was far from over. The organization was still a formidable enemy, and they needed to remain vigilant and prepared for whatever challenges lay ahead.

Senator Carter's support proved invaluable as they continued their efforts to dismantle The Syndicate. Her position within the government provided them with access to critical information and resources, and her dedication to justice inspired them to persevere. Together, they formed a powerful alliance, committed to exposing corruption and bringing those responsible to justice.

As they planned their next moves, Alex couldn't shake the feeling that The Handler was still watching, still pulling the strings from behind the scenes. The true identity and motives of The Handler remained shrouded in mystery, and Alex knew that uncovering the truth would be crucial to their mission.

Sarah, too, was determined to find out who The Handler really was. Her investigation had brought her closer to the heart of the conspiracy, but she knew that there were still many unanswered questions. Together, she and Alex vowed to uncover the truth, no matter the cost.

The next phase of their mission would be the most challenging yet, but Alex and Sarah were ready. They had faced incredible odds and emerged victorious, and they knew that the battle for Veridan's soul was far from over. Together, they would continue to fight for justice, exposing the shadows of power and dismantling the web of deceit that had ensnared their city.

As they looked out over the city, Alex and Sarah felt a renewed sense of purpose. They had played a dangerous game, but they had emerged stronger and more determined than ever. And they knew that as long as there were puppet masters pulling the strings, they would continue to fight for a future free from corruption and control. The battle was far from over, but they were ready to face whatever dangers came their way, knowing that the pursuit of justice was a journey that never truly ended.

The days following Blackwood's assassination were marked by heightened tension and increased security measures across Veridan. The Syndicate, reeling from the loss of one of their key operatives, responded with a crackdown on suspected threats and a tightening of their internal security. Alex and Sarah had anticipated this reaction and took extra precautions to avoid detection.

Their next target, a high-ranking politician with close ties to The Syndicate, was someone who wielded significant influence in Veridan's government. This individual had been instrumental in passing legislation that benefited The Syndicate's corporate backers and had used their position to shield the organization from scrutiny. Alex and Sarah knew that taking down this politician would deal a significant blow to The Syndicate's operations.

As they gathered intelligence on their new target, Alex and Sarah continued to work closely together, sharing information and coordinating their efforts. They were acutely aware of the dangers they faced, but their resolve was unwavering. They had come too far to turn back now, and they were determined to see their mission through to the end.

Sarah's investigation had uncovered more details about The Syndicate's structure and operations.

She had identified several key figures within the organization, including financiers, strategists, and enforcers. This information provided valuable insights into The Syndicate's inner workings and helped Alex and Sarah plan their next moves.

One evening, as they reviewed their findings, Sarah received a tip from one of her trusted sources. The tip indicated that The Syndicate's leadership would be holding a secret meeting to discuss their next steps in response to Blackwood's assassination. The meeting was set to take place at a secure location in the heart of the city, and the source provided the time and address.

Alex and Sarah knew that this was a rare opportunity to gather intelligence and possibly eliminate multiple high-ranking members of The Syndicate in one fell swoop. They began to formulate a plan to infiltrate the meeting and record the proceedings, with the goal of using the evidence to expose the organization's activities.

The location of the meeting was a luxurious penthouse in one of Veridan's most exclusive neighborhoods. The building had state-of-the-art security, including biometric access controls, surveillance cameras, and armed guards. Alex and Sarah knew that gaining access would be challenging, but they were determined to succeed.

On the night of the meeting, Alex and Sarah arrived at the building, using disguises to blend in with the other residents and visitors. Alex had obtained a stolen access card from a contact, which allowed them to bypass the initial security checkpoint. They took the elevator to the top floor, their hearts pounding with anticipation.

As they approached the penthouse, Alex used a device to hack into the building's security system, temporarily disabling the cameras and alarms. They moved quickly and silently, reaching the door to the penthouse without being detected. Alex picked the lock with practiced ease, and they slipped inside.

The penthouse was lavishly decorated, with floor-to-ceiling windows offering stunning views of the city. In the center of the living room, a group of well-dressed individuals sat around a large table, deep in discussion. Alex and Sarah recognized several of them as key figures within The Syndicate, including their current target, the high-ranking politician.

Alex set up a small camera to record the meeting, positioning it discreetly behind a decorative sculpture. He and Sarah then took up positions where they could listen and observe without being seen. The leaders of The Syndicate were discussing their plans in response to the recent events, including strategies to protect their interests and counter the actions of Alex and Sarah.

The conversation revealed the full extent of The Syndicate's influence and their willingness to use any means necessary to achieve their goals. They discussed bribing officials, manipulating media coverage, and even resorting to violence to maintain control. It was clear that The Syndicate was a formidable and ruthless organization, willing to go to any lengths to protect their power.

As the meeting continued, Alex and Sarah's presence was suddenly detected. One of the security guards had noticed the disabled cameras and raised the alarm. The leaders of The Syndicate reacted quickly, ordering their guards to secure the penthouse and find the intruders.

Alex and Sarah knew they had to act fast. They retrieved the camera and made their way to the nearest exit, but they were confronted by armed guards. A fierce firefight ensued, with Alex and Sarah using their training and skills to fight their way out. Bullets flew, and the sounds of gunfire echoed through the penthouse.

Despite the overwhelming odds, Alex and Sarah managed to escape, but not without injuries. They made their way to a safe house, where they treated their wounds and reviewed the footage they had captured. The evidence was damning, providing clear proof of The Syndicate's activities and their plans to manipulate political events.

With the footage in hand, Alex and Sarah contacted their allies in the media and law enforcement, arranging for a coordinated release of the information. The story broke the next day, sending shockwaves through Veridan and beyond. The public was stunned by the revelations, and calls for accountability grew louder.

The government launched a comprehensive investigation into The Syndicate, resulting in the arrest of several key figures and the seizure of their assets. The organization's influence began to wane, and their grip on Veridan weakened. The successful operation had dealt a significant blow to The Syndicate, but Alex and Sarah knew that their work was far from over.

As the city continued to grapple with the fallout from the revelations, Alex and Sarah remained focused on their mission. They had exposed the puppet masters who had been manipulating political events, but they knew that there were still threats to be eliminated and secrets to be uncovered.

The battle against The Syndicate was not yet won, but Alex and Sarah were ready to face whatever challenges lay ahead. Their resolve was stronger than ever, and they were determined to continue fighting for justice and a future free from corruption and control. As they looked out over the city, they felt a renewed sense of purpose, knowing that the pursuit of justice was a journey that never truly ended.

The successful assassination of General Victor Blackwood had sent a clear message: The Syndicate was not invincible, and their grip on Veridan was beginning to slip. As the city continued to grapple with the fallout from the recent events, Alex and Sarah remained focused on their mission. They were determined to expose the puppet masters who had been manipulating political events and bring them to justice.

The next phase of their mission would be the most challenging yet, but Alex and Sarah were ready. They had faced incredible odds and emerged victorious, and they knew that the battle for Veridan's soul was far from over. Together, they would continue to fight for justice, exposing the shadows of power and dismantling the web of deceit that had ensnared their city.

As they looked out over the city, Alex and Sarah felt a renewed sense of purpose. They had played a dangerous game, but they had emerged stronger and more determined than ever. And they knew that as long as there were puppet masters pulling the strings, they would continue to fight for a future free from corruption and control. The battle was far from over, but they were ready to face whatever dangers came their way, knowing that the pursuit of justice was a journey that never truly ended.

The days following Blackwood's assassination were marked by heightened tension and increased security measures across Veridan. The Syndicate, reeling from the loss of one of their key operatives, responded with a crackdown on suspected threats and a tightening of their internal security. Alex and Sarah had anticipated this reaction and took extra precautions to avoid detection.

Their next target, a high-ranking politician with close ties to The Syndicate, was someone who wielded significant influence in Veridan's government. This individual had been instrumental in passing legislation that benefited The Syndicate's corporate backers and had used their position to shield the organization from scrutiny. Alex and Sarah knew that taking down this politician would deal a significant blow to The Syndicate's operations.

As they gathered intelligence on their new target, Alex and Sarah continued to work closely together, sharing information and coordinating their efforts. They were acutely aware of the dangers they faced, but their resolve was unwavering. They had come too far to turn back now, and they were determined to see their mission through to the end.

Sarah's investigation had uncovered more details about The Syndicate's structure and operations. She had identified several key figures within the organization, including financiers, strategists, and enforcers. This information provided valuable insights into The Syndicate's inner workings and helped Alex and Sarah plan their next moves.

One evening, as they reviewed their findings, Sarah received a tip from one of her trusted sources. The tip indicated that The Syndicate's leadership would be holding a secret meeting to discuss their next steps in response to Blackwood's assassination. The meeting was set to take place at a secure location in the heart of the city, and the source provided the time and address.

Alex and Sarah knew that this was a rare opportunity to gather intelligence and possibly eliminate multiple high-ranking members of The Syndicate in one fell swoop. They began to formulate a plan to infiltrate the meeting and record the proceedings, with the goal of using the evidence to expose the organization's activities.

The location of the meeting was a luxurious penthouse in one of Veridan's most exclusive neighborhoods. The building had state-of-the-art security, including biometric access controls, surveillance cameras, and armed guards. Alex and Sarah knew that gaining access would be challenging, but they were determined to succeed.

On the night of the meeting, Alex and Sarah arrived at the building, using disguises to blend in with the other residents and visitors. Alex had obtained a stolen access card from a contact, which allowed them to bypass the initial security checkpoint. They took the elevator to the top floor, their hearts pounding with anticipation.

As they approached the penthouse, Alex used a device to hack into the building's security system, temporarily disabling the cameras and alarms. They moved quickly and silently, reaching the door to the penthouse without being detected. Alex picked the lock with practiced ease, and they slipped inside.

The penthouse was lavishly decorated, with floor-to-ceiling windows offering stunning views of the city. In the center of the living room, a group of well-dressed individuals sat around a large table, deep in discussion. Alex and Sarah recognized several of them as key figures within The Syndicate, including their current target, the high-ranking politician.

Alex set up a small camera to record the meeting, positioning it discreetly behind a decorative sculpture. He and Sarah then took up positions where they could listen and observe without being seen. The leaders of The Syndicate were discussing their plans in response to the recent events, including strategies to protect their interests and counter the actions of Alex and Sarah.

The conversation revealed the full extent of The Syndicate's influence and their willingness to use any means necessary to achieve their goals. They discussed bribing officials, manipulating media coverage, and even resorting to violence to maintain control. It was clear that The Syndicate was a formidable and ruthless organization, willing to go to any lengths to protect their power.

As the meeting continued, Alex and Sarah's presence was suddenly detected. One of the security guards had noticed the disabled cameras and raised the alarm. The leaders of The Syndicate reacted quickly, ordering their guards to secure the penthouse and find the intruders.

Alex and Sarah knew they had to act fast. They retrieved the camera and made their way to the nearest exit, but they were confronted by armed guards. A fierce firefight ensued, with Alex and Sarah using their training and skills to fight their way out. Bullets flew, and the sounds of gunfire echoed through the penthouse.

Despite the overwhelming odds, Alex and Sarah managed to escape, but not without injuries. They made their way to a safe house, where they treated their wounds and reviewed the footage they had captured. The evidence was damning, providing clear proof of The Syndicate's activities and their plans to manipulate political events.

With the footage in hand, Alex and Sarah contacted their allies in the media and law enforcement, arranging for a coordinated release of the information. The story broke the next day, sending shockwaves through Veridan and beyond. The public was stunned by the revelations, and calls for accountability grew louder.

The government launched a comprehensive investigation into The Syndicate, resulting in the arrest of several key figures and the seizure of their assets. The organization's influence began to wane, and their grip on Veridan weakened. The successful operation had dealt a significant blow to The Syndicate, but Alex and Sarah knew that their work was far from over.

As the city continued to grapple with the fallout from the revelations, Alex and Sarah remained focused on their mission. They had exposed the puppet masters who had been manipulating political events, but they knew that there were still threats to be eliminated and secrets to be uncovered.

The battle against The Syndicate was not yet won, but Alex and Sarah were ready to face whatever challenges lay ahead. Their resolve was stronger than ever, and they were determined to continue fighting for justice and a future free from corruption and control. As they looked out over the city, they felt a renewed sense of purpose, knowing that the pursuit of justice was a journey that never truly ended.

The successful assassination of General Victor Blackwood had sent a clear message: The Syndicate was not invincible, and their grip on Veridan was beginning to slip. As the city continued to grapple with the fallout from the recent events, Alex and Sarah remained focused on their mission. They were determined to expose the puppet masters who had been manipulating political events and bring them to justice.

The next phase of their mission would be the most challenging yet, but Alex and Sarah were ready. They had faced incredible odds and emerged victorious, and they knew that the battle for Veridan's soul was far from over. Together, they would continue to fight for justice, exposing the shadows of power and dismantling the web of deceit that had ensnared their city.

As they looked out over the city, Alex and Sarah felt a renewed sense of purpose. They had played a dangerous game, but they had emerged stronger and more determined than ever. And they knew that as long as there were puppet masters pulling the strings, they would continue to fight for a future free from corruption and control. The battle was far from over, but they were ready to face whatever dangers came their way, knowing that the pursuit of justice was a journey that never truly ended.

Chapter 9: Crossroads

The city of Veridan was in upheaval. The once-invisible Syndicate was now exposed, their corruption and manipulation laid bare for all to see. The public was outraged, demanding justice and sweeping reforms. As the government's investigation into the Syndicate intensified, so did their efforts to capture the elusive assassin responsible for the deaths of high-ranking officials. Alex Morgan found himself at a crossroads, grappling with his role in this deadly game and the moral boundaries he was crossing.

As he stared out over the city from his safe house, Alex's mind was a storm of conflicting emotions. He had always believed that his actions were justified, that he was striking against those who sought to harm Veridan. But with each mission, the lines between right and wrong became increasingly blurred. The realization that he was being manipulated by The Handler gnawed at him, raising questions about the true motives behind his assignments.

Alex's thoughts were interrupted by the sound of the door opening. Sarah Mitchell entered, carrying a stack of papers and a determined expression. She had just published her most explosive exposé yet, detailing the inner workings of the Syndicate and the complicity of key figures in the government and corporate world. The article had hit the newsstands that morning, and the reaction was immediate and intense.

Sarah dropped the papers on the table and sank into a chair, her exhaustion evident. "It's out there, Alex. Everything we've uncovered. The public is furious, and the government is scrambling to respond. This is our chance to make real change."

Alex nodded, but his mind was still preoccupied with his own internal struggle. "I know, Sarah. But at what cost? I've killed people, manipulated events, and all under the guidance of someone whose true intentions I don't even understand. What if we're just pawns in a larger game?"

Sarah leaned forward, her eyes filled with determination. "We may be pawns, Alex, but we're making a difference. We've exposed the Syndicate, and we're holding them accountable. Yes, it's dangerous, and yes, it's morally complex, but we can't stop now. We owe it to the people of Veridan to see this through."

Alex sighed, running a hand through his hair. "I understand, but I can't help but feel conflicted. The more I dig, the more I question my role in all of this. Am I really fighting for justice, or am I just another tool for someone else's agenda?"

Sarah reached out and placed a hand on his arm. "You're fighting for justice, Alex. Whatever The Handler's motives are, you've made a choice to stand up against corruption and abuse of power. Don't lose sight of that. We still have work to do."

Their conversation was interrupted by the sound of sirens in the distance. The government's efforts to capture Alex had intensified, and the net was closing in. They both knew that staying in one place for too long was risky, but they needed to plan their next move carefully.

Alex pulled out a map of the city and spread it across the table. "Our next target is Lawrence Whitaker, the Syndicate's financial mastermind. Taking him down will cripple their operations and expose the flow of money that fuels their corruption. But he's heavily guarded, and we'll need a solid plan to get to him."

Sarah nodded, her mind already working through the logistics. "Whitaker has a private estate on the outskirts of the city. It's a fortress, but there are always weaknesses. We need to gather intel on his security measures, his routine, and find a way in."

As they discussed their strategy, Alex couldn't shake the feeling that they were running out of time. The government's hunt for him was relentless, and the Syndicate was still a powerful enemy. But he also knew that this mission was critical. Taking down Whitaker could be the turning point they needed to dismantle the Syndicate for good.

Over the next few days, Alex and Sarah worked tirelessly to gather information on Whitaker. They hacked into his financial records, monitored his communications, and conducted surveillance on his estate. Every detail was scrutinized, every possible angle considered. The plan was to infiltrate the estate during a high-profile charity event that Whitaker was hosting. The event would provide cover and allow Alex to get close enough to Whitaker to execute the mission.

The night of the event arrived, and Alex and Sarah were ready. They had acquired invitations through their network of contacts, allowing them to blend in with the other guests. Dressed in formal attire, they approached the estate with confidence, their minds focused on the task at hand.

The estate was a sprawling property, surrounded by high walls and patrolled by armed guards. Inside, the guests mingled in opulent surroundings, unaware of the danger that lurked among them. Alex and Sarah moved through the crowd, their eyes scanning for Whitaker.

Whitaker was easy to spot, holding court in the center of the room, surrounded by influential figures from the business and political world. He exuded confidence and charm, but Alex could see the calculating mind behind the facade. This was a man who thrived on power and control, and his downfall would send a powerful message.

As the evening progressed, Alex and Sarah executed their plan with precision. Sarah engaged Whitaker in conversation, distracting him while Alex prepared for the hit. He positioned himself in a secluded area, waiting for the right moment to strike.

The opportunity came when Whitaker excused himself to make a private phone call. Alex followed him to a quiet hallway, his heart pounding with anticipation. Whitaker was alone, his guard down. Alex approached silently, his silenced pistol ready.

"Whitaker," Alex said, his voice steady. "It's over."

Whitaker turned, his eyes widening in surprise. "Who are you?"

"The end of the line," Alex replied, pulling the trigger. The shot was precise, and Whitaker fell to the ground, his life extinguished.

Alex quickly searched Whitaker's pockets, retrieving a keycard and a small notebook. The keycard provided access to Whitaker's private office, a treasure trove of information that could further expose the Syndicate. The notebook contained cryptic notes and contacts, a glimpse into the network of power and corruption that Whitaker had cultivated.

As Alex made his way back to the main room, he signaled to Sarah. They needed to leave quickly before the alarm was raised. They exited the estate and disappeared into the night, their mission successful.

Back at the safe house, Alex and Sarah reviewed the information they had gathered. The keycard granted them access to Whitaker's private server, revealing detailed financial records and communications that linked the Syndicate to key figures in the government and corporate world. The evidence was damning, providing a clear picture of the Syndicate's operations and their plans to manipulate political events.

Sarah worked tirelessly to compile the information into a comprehensive report, while Alex monitored their security and prepared for the next steps. The report was sent to trusted media outlets and government officials, ensuring that the information would be widely disseminated and acted upon.

The following day, the story broke, sending shockwaves through Veridan. The public was outraged by the revelations, and calls for accountability grew louder. The government launched a comprehensive investigation into the Syndicate, resulting in the arrest of several key figures and the seizure of their assets. The organization's influence began to wane, and their grip on Veridan weakened.

As the city continued to grapple with the fallout from the revelations, Alex and Sarah remained focused on their mission. They had exposed the puppet masters who had been manipulating political events, but they knew that there were still threats to be eliminated and secrets to be uncovered.

The successful operation against Whitaker had dealt a significant blow to the Syndicate, but Alex and Sarah knew that their work was far from over. The organization was still a formidable enemy, and they needed to remain vigilant and prepared for whatever challenges lay ahead.

Senator Carter's support proved invaluable as they continued their efforts to dismantle the Syndicate. Her position within the government provided them with access to critical information and resources, and her dedication to justice inspired them to persevere. Together, they formed a powerful alliance, committed to exposing corruption and bringing those responsible to justice.

As they planned their next moves, Alex couldn't shake the feeling that The Handler was still watching, still pulling the strings from behind the scenes. The true identity and motives of The Handler remained shrouded in mystery, and Alex knew that uncovering the truth would be crucial to their mission.

Sarah, too, was determined to find out who The Handler really was. Her investigation had brought her closer to the heart of the conspiracy, but she knew that there were still many unanswered questions. Together, she and Alex vowed to uncover the truth, no matter the cost.

The next phase of their mission would be the most challenging yet, but Alex and Sarah were ready. They had faced incredible odds and emerged victorious, and they knew that the battle for Veridan's soul was far from over. Together, they would continue to fight for justice, exposing the shadows of power and dismantling the web of deceit that had ensnared their city.

As they looked out over the city, Alex and Sarah felt a renewed sense of purpose. They had played a dangerous game, but they had emerged stronger and more determined than ever. And they knew that as long as there were puppet masters pulling the strings, they would continue to fight for a future free from corruption and control. The battle was far from over, but they were ready to face whatever dangers came their way, knowing that the pursuit of justice was a journey that never truly ended.

Chapter 10: The Financial Web

Veridan was in a state of turmoil, grappling with the fallout from the recent exposures of the Syndicate. The public outcry and subsequent government investigations had rocked the foundations of the city's political and economic landscape. Amidst this chaos, Alex Morgan and Sarah Mitchell continued their relentless pursuit of justice, each driven by a burning desire to dismantle the Syndicate and bring its leaders to account.

Lawrence Whitaker, the Syndicate's financial mastermind, was their next target. Known for his cunning and ruthless approach to finance, Whitaker was instrumental in orchestrating the Syndicate's economic strategies, using his vast network of connections to manipulate markets and amass wealth. Taking him down would not only disrupt the Syndicate's financial operations but also send a powerful message to those who believed themselves untouchable.

Alex had been meticulously planning the infiltration of Whitaker's high-security mansion for weeks. The mansion, located in an exclusive neighborhood on the outskirts of Veridan, was a fortress. It was equipped with state-of-the-art security systems, guarded by a private security team, and surrounded by a high wall with surveillance cameras at every corner. The task ahead was daunting, but Alex was undeterred.

Using his network of contacts, Alex gathered intelligence on Whitaker's security measures, daily routines, and the layout of the mansion. Every detail was scrutinized and incorporated into his plan. He knew that timing and precision were crucial. The plan was to infiltrate the mansion during a high-profile business gathering that Whitaker was hosting. The event would provide the cover Alex needed to get close to his target.

The night of the event arrived, and Alex was ready. Disguised as a waiter, he approached the mansion with a sense of calm determination. His cover allowed him to blend in seamlessly with the staff, giving him access to the interior of the mansion without raising suspicion. As he moved through the lavishly decorated halls, his eyes constantly scanned for security personnel and surveillance cameras.

Inside, the mansion was a hive of activity. The business elite of Veridan mingled, discussing investments and strategies, oblivious to the danger in their midst. Whitaker held court in the grand hall, his presence commanding and confident. Alex watched from a distance, waiting for the right moment to strike.

As the evening progressed, Alex made his way to the mansion's security control room. Using a forged keycard, he gained access and quickly disabled the security cameras and alarm systems. With the mansion's defenses temporarily compromised, he moved swiftly towards Whitaker's private office.

Whitaker's office was a testament to his wealth and power. The walls were lined with bookshelves filled with financial tomes, and the desk was adorned with expensive artifacts and personal mementos. Alex began to search for any documents or digital files that could reveal the Syndicate's plans. He hacked into Whitaker's computer, downloading files and transferring data to a secure drive.

As he sifted through the documents, Alex uncovered detailed plans to destabilize Veridan's economy. The Syndicate intended to manipulate stock markets, create artificial shortages of essential goods, and orchestrate financial crises to weaken the government and force policy changes that would benefit their interests. The scale and audacity of the plan were staggering, revealing the depths of the Syndicate's ambitions.

With the evidence in hand, Alex knew he had to act quickly. He made his way back to the grand hall, where Whitaker was still entertaining his guests. As he approached, he drew his silenced pistol, his movements calculated and deliberate. He reached Whitaker just as the financier was raising a toast, his voice booming through the hall.

"Ladies and gentlemen, to our continued success and prosperity!" Whitaker declared, unaware of the danger behind him.

Alex stepped forward, his voice low and steady. "Lawrence Whitaker, your time is up."

The shot was fired with precision, the sound barely audible over the clinking of glasses and murmurs of conversation. Whitaker's body crumpled to the floor, the glass falling from his hand and shattering. For a moment, there was stunned silence, followed by a wave of panic as guests realized what had happened.

Amidst the chaos, Alex moved swiftly towards the exit. The security systems were still down, giving him a crucial window to escape. He navigated through the panicked crowd, slipping out of the mansion and disappearing into the night.

The assassination of Lawrence Whitaker sent shockwaves through Veridan and the global financial markets. News of his death spread quickly, causing panic among investors and triggering a market downturn. The government responded with an immediate investigation, and financial institutions scrambled to contain the fallout.

Back at the safe house, Alex reviewed the data he had retrieved from Whitaker's computer. The evidence was damning, providing a clear picture of the Syndicate's plans to destabilize the economy. He knew that releasing this information would further expose the Syndicate's operations and cripple their ability to manipulate markets.

As Alex prepared to send the data to trusted media outlets and government officials, he received an unexpected visitor. Sarah Mitchell entered the room, her expression one of urgency and determination.

"Alex, we need to talk," she said, her voice steady but urgent.

Alex looked up, recognizing the intensity in her eyes. "Sarah, what's going on?"

"I've been following the fallout from Whitaker's assassination, and it's worse than we anticipated. The Syndicate is retaliating, using their remaining influence to target key figures in the government and media. We need to act fast and release this information before they can do more damage."

Alex nodded, realizing the gravity of the situation. "You're right. We need to expose their plans and cut off their ability to operate."

Together, Alex and Sarah compiled the data into a comprehensive report, detailing the Syndicate's financial manipulations and their plans to destabilize the economy. They sent the report to multiple media outlets and government agencies, ensuring that the information would be widely disseminated and acted upon.

As the story broke, public outrage reached a fever pitch. The revelations about the Syndicate's plans to manipulate the economy and weaken the government galvanized the public, leading to massive protests and demands for justice. The government intensified its efforts to dismantle the Syndicate, launching raids and arresting key figures associated with the organization.

The financial markets, initially shaken by Whitaker's assassination, began to stabilize as confidence in the government's response grew. Measures were put in place to safeguard the economy and prevent further manipulation by the Syndicate. The public's faith in the financial system, though shaken, was gradually being restored.

For Alex and Sarah, the success of their mission was a significant victory, but they knew that their work was far from over. The Syndicate was still a formidable enemy, and they needed to remain vigilant and prepared for whatever challenges lay ahead.

As they sat together in the safe house, reflecting on their journey, Alex felt a renewed sense of purpose. He had faced his doubts and questions, but now he was more determined than ever to continue the fight for justice.

"Sarah, we've made significant progress, but there's still a lot of work to do. The Syndicate is weakened, but they're not defeated. We need to stay focused and keep pushing forward."

Sarah nodded, her eyes filled with resolve. "I agree, Alex. We've come too far to stop now. We need to keep exposing their operations and bring the remaining leaders to justice."

Their conversation was interrupted by the sound of a message alert on Alex's phone. It was from The Handler, the enigmatic figure who had guided Alex through his missions. The message was brief and cryptic, as always:

"Well done, Alex. Whitaker's death and the exposure of the Syndicate's plans have dealt a significant blow to the organization. Your next target will be provided soon. Stay vigilant."

Alex showed the message to Sarah, his expression one of determination. "The Handler is still guiding us, but I can't shake the feeling that there's more to this than we realize. We need to find out who The Handler really is and understand their true motives."

Sarah agreed, her mind already working through the possibilities. "I've been digging into The Handler's communications and trying to trace their origins. It's not easy, but I believe we can find some answers if we keep pushing."

As they prepared for the next phase of their mission, Alex and Sarah knew that the road ahead would be perilous. The Syndicate was a formidable enemy, and uncovering The Handler's true identity would add another layer of complexity to their efforts. But they were ready to face whatever challenges came their way, driven by their shared commitment to justice and the pursuit of truth.

In the days that followed, Alex and Sarah continued to gather intelligence on the Syndicate and its remaining leaders. They uncovered more details about the organization's operations, financial transactions, and connections to key figures in the government and corporate world. The more they learned, the clearer it became that the Syndicate was deeply entrenched in Veridan's power structure.

Their investigation also led them to discover a network of safe houses and hideouts used by the Syndicate's operatives. These locations provided valuable information and resources that helped Alex and Sarah in their mission. They conducted raids, gathered evidence, and dismantled the Syndicate's infrastructure piece by piece.

One evening, as they reviewed their findings, Sarah received a tip from one of her trusted sources. The tip indicated that the Syndicate's remaining leaders were planning a high-level meeting to discuss their next steps and regroup after the recent setbacks. The meeting was set to take place at a remote location, far from the prying eyes of the public.

Alex and Sarah knew that this was a rare opportunity to gather intelligence and possibly eliminate multiple high-ranking members of the Syndicate in one fell swoop. They began to formulate a plan to infiltrate the meeting and record the proceedings, with the goal of using the evidence to expose the organization's activities.

The location of the meeting was a secluded mansion in the countryside, surrounded by dense forests and accessible only by a single road. The mansion was heavily guarded, with multiple layers of security and a contingent of armed guards. Alex and Sarah knew that gaining access would be challenging, but they were determined to succeed.

On the night of the meeting, Alex and Sarah arrived at the location, using disguises to blend in with the staff and guests. Alex had obtained a forged invitation, allowing them to pass through the initial security checkpoint. They took a back entrance to the mansion, their hearts pounding with anticipation.

As they approached the mansion, Alex used a device to hack into the security system, temporarily disabling the cameras and alarms. They moved quickly and silently, reaching the main hall where the meeting was taking place. The leaders of the Syndicate were gathered around a large table, deep in discussion.

Alex and Sarah positioned themselves discreetly, setting up cameras and recording devices to capture the conversation. The leaders were discussing their plans to recover from the recent setbacks, including strategies to protect their remaining assets and counter the actions of Alex and Sarah.

The conversation revealed the full extent of the Syndicate's influence and their willingness to use any means necessary to achieve their goals. They discussed bribing officials, manipulating media coverage, and even resorting to violence to maintain control. It was clear that the Syndicate was a formidable and ruthless organization, willing to go to any lengths to protect their power.

As the meeting continued, Alex and Sarah's presence was suddenly detected. One of the security guards had noticed the disabled cameras and raised the alarm. The leaders of the Syndicate reacted quickly, ordering their guards to secure the mansion and find the intruders.

Alex and Sarah knew they had to act fast. They retrieved the cameras and made their way to the nearest exit, but they were confronted by armed guards. A fierce firefight ensued, with Alex and Sarah using their training and skills to fight their way out. Bullets flew, and the sounds of gunfire echoed through the mansion.

Despite the overwhelming odds, Alex and Sarah managed to escape, but not without injuries. They made their way to a safe house, where they treated their wounds and reviewed the footage they had captured. The evidence was damning, providing clear proof of the Syndicate's activities and their plans to manipulate political events.

With the footage in hand, Alex and Sarah contacted their allies in the media and law enforcement, arranging for a coordinated release of the information. The story broke the next day, sending shockwaves through Veridan and beyond. The public was stunned by the revelations, and calls for accountability grew louder.

The government launched a comprehensive investigation into the Syndicate, resulting in the arrest of several key figures and the seizure of their assets. The organization's influence began to wane, and their grip on Veridan weakened. The successful operation had dealt a significant blow to the Syndicate, but Alex and Sarah knew that their work was far from over.

As the city continued to grapple with the fallout from the revelations, Alex and Sarah remained focused on their mission. They had exposed the puppet masters who had been manipulating political events, but they knew that there were still threats to be eliminated and secrets to be uncovered.

The battle against the Syndicate was not yet won, but Alex and Sarah were ready to face whatever challenges lay ahead. Their resolve was stronger than ever, and they were determined to continue fighting for justice and a future free from corruption and control. As they looked out over the city, they felt a renewed sense of purpose, knowing that the pursuit of justice was a journey that never truly ended.

Chapter 11: Allies and Adversaries

The city of Veridan was in a state of upheaval as the Syndicate's nefarious activities were being brought to light. The public outcry, coupled with government investigations, had left the city's power structure shaken. Amidst this chaos, Alex Morgan and Sarah Mitchell found themselves forming an uneasy but necessary alliance. Both driven by their desire for justice, they knew that working together was their best chance to dismantle the Syndicate and expose its leaders.

Despite their shared goal, there was an underlying tension between them. Alex, a skilled assassin with a shadowy past, was used to operating alone, driven by his own code of justice. Sarah, an intrepid investigative journalist, was driven by her commitment to uncovering the truth and holding the powerful accountable. Their methods differed significantly, and this difference often led to friction.

One evening, in the relative safety of their current hideout, Alex and Sarah sat down to discuss their next move. The room was dimly lit, the atmosphere heavy with the weight of their mission.

"We've made significant progress," Sarah began, her tone serious. "But we need to keep the momentum going. The Syndicate is still a formidable enemy, and they're regrouping."

Alex nodded, his expression grim. "Agreed. We need to strike while they're still reeling from Whitaker's death. Our next target is crucial."

Sarah pulled out a dossier from her bag and spread it out on the table. "Senator Rachel Hayes. She's the Syndicate's political liaison, the one who's been ensuring their interests are protected within the government. Taking her down will disrupt their political influence and expose more of their operations."

Alex studied the dossier, noting Hayes' connections and the power she wielded. "She's heavily guarded and well-connected. We need to gather more evidence before we can make a move."

Sarah nodded. "I've been working on that. I have a contact within Hayes' inner circle, someone who's willing to provide us with information in exchange for protection. We need to arrange a meeting."

As they planned their next steps, the tension between them was palpable. Their alliance was uneasy, born out of necessity rather than trust. But both knew that they couldn't succeed without each other.

Over the next few days, Alex and Sarah worked tirelessly to gather evidence against Senator Hayes. Sarah's contact, a former aide to Hayes, provided them with valuable information about her dealings with the Syndicate. The aide revealed that Hayes was scheduled to attend a secret meeting with several high-ranking Syndicate members, where they would discuss their next moves in response to the recent setbacks.

Armed with this information, Alex and Sarah devised a plan to intercept the meeting and gather irrefutable evidence. The meeting was to take place at a secluded estate outside the city, a location that provided both privacy and security for the Syndicate members.

On the night of the meeting, Alex and Sarah arrived at the estate, using their network of contacts to gain access. They moved stealthily through the grounds, avoiding the guards and surveillance cameras. As they approached the main building, they overheard snippets of conversation that confirmed their suspicions: the Syndicate was planning a series of coordinated actions to regain control and counter the government's investigation.

Inside, the atmosphere was tense. The Syndicate's leaders, including Senator Hayes, were deep in discussion, their faces etched with concern and determination. Alex and Sarah positioned themselves in a hidden alcove, recording the conversation with a concealed device.

Hayes was at the center of the discussion, her voice authoritative and confident. "We need to act swiftly and decisively. The recent setbacks have weakened us, but we can still turn this around. We have allies within the government and the corporate world. We need to leverage those connections and strike back."

The other members nodded in agreement, their expressions grim. They discussed plans to manipulate media coverage, bribe officials, and use their financial resources to create economic instability. It was clear that the Syndicate was far from defeated and that their influence extended deep into the fabric of Veridan's society.

As Alex and Sarah continued to listen, they realized the full extent of the Syndicate's reach. This was not just a group of corrupt individuals; it was a well-organized network with the power to manipulate events on a grand scale. The evidence they were gathering was damning, but they needed to ensure that it reached the right people.

After the meeting concluded, Alex and Sarah made their way back to their hideout, their minds racing with the implications of what they had heard. They reviewed the recordings, confirming that they had captured enough evidence to expose the Syndicate's plans and their connections to key figures in the government.

The next step was to compile the evidence into a comprehensive report and distribute it to trusted media outlets and government officials. This would ensure that the information was widely disseminated and acted upon, preventing the Syndicate from using their influence to suppress the truth.

As they worked on the report, Alex couldn't shake the feeling that their alliance was becoming more than just a partnership of convenience. Despite their differences, he had come to respect Sarah's dedication and tenacity. She, in turn, had come to appreciate Alex's skills and his unwavering commitment to justice.

Their work was interrupted by the arrival of a message from The Handler. The screen flickered to life, displaying the now-familiar cryptic message:

"Well done, Alex. The evidence you've gathered will deal a significant blow to the Syndicate. Your next target is Senator Rachel Hayes. Her removal will further weaken their political influence. Stay vigilant."

Alex showed the message to Sarah, his expression serious. "The Handler wants us to take out Hayes. This will be our most challenging mission yet."

Sarah nodded, her eyes reflecting a mixture of determination and concern. "We need to be careful. Hayes is well-protected, and any misstep could expose us. But if we succeed, it will cripple the Syndicate's political operations."

They continued to work on their plan, aware that time was of the essence. The Syndicate was regrouping, and their window of opportunity was closing. They needed to act quickly and decisively to ensure that their mission was successful.

The night of the operation arrived, and Alex and Sarah were ready. They had gathered intelligence on Hayes' security measures, her routine, and the layout of her residence. Every detail had been meticulously planned, and they knew that this mission would require precision, timing, and a bit of luck.

Dressed in black and equipped with the necessary tools, Alex and Sarah made their way to Hayes' residence. The mansion was located in an exclusive neighborhood, surrounded by high walls and patrolled by armed guards. They approached from the rear, using the cover of darkness to avoid detection.

Alex disabled the security systems with a device, creating a temporary window to slip past the perimeter defenses. They moved swiftly and silently, making their way to the main building. Inside, they navigated the corridors, avoiding the guards and surveillance cameras.

As they reached Hayes' private quarters, they encountered several guards. A brief but intense firefight ensued, with Alex and Sarah using their training and skills to neutralize the threats. They moved quickly, aware that any delay could jeopardize the mission.

Hayes was in her study, reviewing documents at her desk. She looked up as Alex and Sarah entered, her eyes widening in surprise. "Who are you?" she demanded, her voice steady but laced with fear.

Alex stepped forward, his expression cold and determined. "Your time is up, Senator Hayes. The Syndicate's reign of terror ends now."

Before Hayes could respond, Alex fired his silenced pistol, the shot echoing softly in the room. Hayes slumped over her desk, her life extinguished. Alex quickly searched the study, retrieving documents and digital files that could provide further evidence of the Syndicate's operations.

As they made their way back to the exit, Alex and Sarah encountered more guards. Another firefight ensued, but they managed to escape, making their way to a waiting vehicle. They drove away from the mansion, their hearts pounding with adrenaline and relief.

Back at their hideout, they reviewed the documents they had retrieved from Hayes' study. The evidence provided further insights into the Syndicate's plans and their connections to key figures in the government. They compiled the information into a comprehensive report, ready to be disseminated to the media and law enforcement.

The assassination of Senator Rachel Hayes sent shockwaves through Veridan's political landscape. The news of her death, coupled with the release of the evidence, sparked a massive public outcry. The government intensified its efforts to dismantle the Syndicate, launching raids and arresting key figures associated with the organization.

As the city continued to grapple with the fallout from the revelations, Alex and Sarah reflected on their journey. Their alliance had been uneasy, but it had proven to be effective. They had exposed the Syndicate's operations, disrupted their plans, and brought key figures to justice. But they knew that their work was far from over.

Alex's thoughts returned to The Handler. The enigmatic figure had guided him through his missions, but their true identity and motives remained a mystery. He knew that uncovering the truth about The Handler would be crucial to their mission.

"Sarah, we've made significant progress, but we still don't know who The Handler is or what their true motives are," Alex said, his tone serious.

Sarah nodded, her expression thoughtful. "I've been digging into The Handler's communications and trying to trace their origins. It's not easy, but I believe we can find some answers if we keep pushing."

As they planned their next moves, Alex and Sarah knew that the road ahead would be perilous. The Syndicate was a formidable enemy, and uncovering The Handler's true identity would add another layer of complexity to their efforts. But they were ready to face whatever challenges came their way, driven by their shared commitment to justice and the pursuit of truth.

In the days that followed, Alex and Sarah continued to gather intelligence on the Syndicate and its remaining leaders. They uncovered more details about the organization's operations, financial transactions, and connections to key figures in the government and corporate world. The more they learned, the clearer it became that the Syndicate was deeply entrenched in Veridan's power structure.

Their investigation also led them to discover a network of safe houses and hideouts used by the Syndicate's operatives. These locations provided valuable information and resources that helped Alex and Sarah in their mission. They conducted raids, gathered evidence, and dismantled the Syndicate's infrastructure piece by piece.

One evening, as they reviewed their findings, Sarah received a tip from one of her trusted sources. The tip indicated that the Syndicate's remaining leaders were planning a high-level meeting to discuss their next steps and regroup after the recent setbacks. The meeting was set to take place at a remote location, far from the prying eyes of the public.

Alex and Sarah knew that this was a rare opportunity to gather intelligence and possibly eliminate multiple high-ranking members of the Syndicate in one fell swoop. They began to formulate a plan to infiltrate the meeting and record the proceedings, with the goal of using the evidence to expose the organization's activities.

The location of the meeting was a secluded mansion in the countryside, surrounded by dense forests and accessible only by a single road. The mansion was heavily guarded, with multiple layers of security and a contingent of armed guards. Alex and Sarah knew that gaining access would be challenging, but they were determined to succeed.

On the night of the meeting, Alex and Sarah arrived at the location, using disguises to blend in with the staff and guests. Alex had obtained a forged invitation, allowing them to pass through the initial security checkpoint. They took a back entrance to the mansion, their hearts pounding with anticipation.

As they approached the mansion, Alex used a device to hack into the security system, temporarily disabling the cameras and alarms. They moved quickly and silently, reaching the main hall where the meeting was taking place. The leaders of the Syndicate were gathered around a large table, deep in discussion.

Alex and Sarah positioned themselves discreetly, setting up cameras and recording devices to capture the conversation. The leaders were discussing their plans to recover from the recent setbacks, including strategies to protect their remaining assets and counter the actions of Alex and Sarah.

The conversation revealed the full extent of the Syndicate's influence and their willingness to use any means necessary to achieve their goals. They discussed bribing officials, manipulating media coverage, and even resorting to violence to maintain control. It was clear that the Syndicate was a formidable and ruthless organization, willing to go to any lengths to protect their power.

As the meeting continued, Alex and Sarah's presence was suddenly detected. One of the security guards had noticed the disabled cameras and raised the alarm. The leaders of the Syndicate reacted quickly, ordering their guards to secure the mansion and find the intruders.

Alex and Sarah knew they had to act fast. They retrieved the cameras and made their way to the nearest exit, but they were confronted by armed guards. A fierce firefight ensued, with Alex and Sarah using their training and skills to fight their way out. Bullets flew, and the sounds of gunfire echoed through the mansion.

Despite the overwhelming odds, Alex and Sarah managed to escape, but not without injuries. They made their way to a safe house, where they treated their wounds and reviewed the footage they had captured. The evidence was damning, providing clear proof of the Syndicate's activities and their plans to manipulate political events.

With the footage in hand, Alex and Sarah contacted their allies in the media and law enforcement, arranging for a coordinated release of the information. The story broke the next day, sending shockwaves through Veridan and beyond. The public was stunned by the revelations, and calls for accountability grew louder.

The government launched a comprehensive investigation into the Syndicate, resulting in the arrest of several key figures and the seizure of their assets. The organization's influence began to wane, and their grip on Veridan weakened. The successful operation had dealt a significant blow to the Syndicate, but Alex and Sarah knew that their work was far from over.

As the city continued to grapple with the fallout from the revelations, Alex and Sarah remained focused on their mission. They had exposed the puppet masters who had been manipulating political events, but they knew that there were still threats to be eliminated and secrets to be uncovered.

The battle against the Syndicate was not yet won, but Alex and Sarah were ready to face whatever challenges lay ahead. Their resolve was stronger than ever, and they were determined to continue fighting for justice and a future free from corruption and control. As they looked out over the city, they felt a renewed sense of purpose, knowing that the pursuit of justice was a journey that never truly ended.

In the days that followed, Alex and Sarah continued to gather intelligence on the Syndicate and its remaining leaders. They uncovered more details about the organization's operations, financial transactions, and connections to key figures in the government and corporate world. The more they learned, the clearer it became that the Syndicate was deeply entrenched in Veridan's power structure.

Their investigation also led them to discover a network of safe houses and hideouts used by the Syndicate's operatives. These locations provided valuable information and resources that helped Alex and Sarah in their mission. They conducted raids, gathered evidence, and dismantled the Syndicate's infrastructure piece by piece.

One evening, as they reviewed their findings, Sarah received a tip from one of her trusted sources. The tip indicated that the Syndicate's remaining leaders were planning a high-level meeting to discuss their next steps and regroup after the recent setbacks. The meeting was set to take place at a remote location, far from the prying eyes of the public.

Alex and Sarah knew that this was a rare opportunity to gather intelligence and possibly eliminate multiple high-ranking members of the Syndicate in one fell swoop. They began to formulate a plan to infiltrate the meeting and record the proceedings, with the goal of using the evidence to expose the organization's activities.

The location of the meeting was a secluded mansion in the countryside, surrounded by dense forests and accessible only by a single road. The mansion was heavily guarded, with multiple layers of security and a contingent of armed guards. Alex and Sarah knew that gaining access would be challenging, but they were determined to succeed.

On the night of the meeting, Alex and Sarah arrived at the location, using disguises to blend in with the staff and guests. Alex had obtained a forged invitation, allowing them to pass through the initial security checkpoint. They took a back entrance to the mansion, their hearts pounding with anticipation.

As they approached the mansion, Alex used a device to hack into the security system, temporarily disabling the cameras and alarms. They moved quickly and silently, reaching the main hall where the meeting was taking place. The leaders of the Syndicate were gathered around a large table, deep in discussion.

Alex and Sarah positioned themselves discreetly, setting up cameras and recording devices to capture the conversation. The leaders were discussing their plans to recover from the recent setbacks, including strategies to protect their remaining assets and counter the actions of Alex and Sarah.

The conversation revealed the full extent of the Syndicate's influence and their willingness to use any means necessary to achieve their goals. They discussed bribing officials, manipulating media coverage, and even resorting to violence to maintain control. It was clear that the Syndicate was a formidable and ruthless organization, willing to go to any lengths to protect their power.

As the meeting continued, Alex and Sarah's presence was suddenly detected. One of the security guards had noticed the disabled cameras and raised the alarm. The leaders of the Syndicate reacted quickly, ordering their guards to secure the mansion and find the intruders.

Alex and Sarah knew they had to act fast. They retrieved the cameras and made their way to the nearest exit, but they were confronted by armed guards. A fierce firefight ensued, with Alex and Sarah using their training and skills to fight their way out. Bullets flew, and the sounds of gunfire echoed through the mansion.

Despite the overwhelming odds, Alex and Sarah managed to escape, but not without injuries. They made their way to a safe house, where they treated their wounds and reviewed the footage they had captured. The evidence was damning, providing clear proof of the Syndicate's activities and their plans to manipulate political events.

With the footage in hand, Alex and Sarah contacted their allies in the media and law enforcement, arranging for a coordinated release of the information. The story broke the next day, sending shockwaves through Veridan and beyond. The public was stunned by the revelations, and calls for accountability grew louder.

The government launched a comprehensive investigation into The Syndicate, resulting in the arrest of several key figures and the seizure of their assets. The organization's influence began to wane, and their grip on Veridan weakened. The successful operation had dealt a significant blow to The Syndicate, but Alex and Sarah knew that their work was far from over.

As the city continued to grapple with the fallout from the revelations, Alex and Sarah remained focused on their mission. They had exposed the puppet masters who had been manipulating political events, but they knew that there were still threats to be eliminated and secrets to be uncovered.

The battle against The Syndicate was not yet won, but Alex and Sarah were ready to face whatever challenges lay ahead. Their resolve was stronger than ever, and they were determined to continue fighting for justice and a future free from corruption and control. As they looked out over the city, they felt a renewed sense of purpose, knowing that the pursuit of justice was a journey that never truly ended.

Chapter 12: The Senator's Secret

The city of Veridan was a cauldron of tension and anticipation as Alex Morgan and Sarah Mitchell moved forward in their mission to dismantle the Syndicate. Their recent victories had shaken the Syndicate's foundation, but they knew that their work was far from over. The next step was to expose Senator Rachel Hayes' deep involvement in the Syndicate's operations and ultimately remove her from the equation.

Senator Hayes had long been suspected of corruption, but concrete evidence had been elusive. Her role within the Syndicate was pivotal, providing the organization with political cover and influence that shielded their illegal activities. Taking her down would strike a significant blow to the Syndicate's political power and further unravel their intricate web of corruption.

Over the past few weeks, Alex and Sarah had meticulously gathered evidence of Hayes' corruption. Sarah's contact within Hayes' inner circle had provided them with critical information about her dealings with the Syndicate, including financial records, communications, and secret meetings. They compiled this evidence into a comprehensive dossier, ready to be released to the public and the authorities.

One evening, as they reviewed the final pieces of evidence, Sarah turned to Alex with a determined expression. "This is it, Alex. We have everything we need to expose Hayes and her ties to the Syndicate. But we need to ensure that the information reaches the right people and that it can't be suppressed."

Alex nodded, his expression serious. "Agreed. We need to distribute the dossier to multiple media outlets and government officials simultaneously. That way, the Syndicate won't be able to stop the truth from coming out."

They spent the next few hours preparing the dossier for distribution, ensuring that it contained all the necessary evidence to prove Hayes' corruption and her connections to the Syndicate. The dossier included financial records showing illegal transactions, emails and text messages detailing her collusion with Syndicate members, and testimony from Sarah's contact, who was willing to go on record.

The following morning, they executed their plan. The dossier was sent to several major media outlets and key figures in the government, including Senator Emily Carter, who had been a staunch ally in their fight against the Syndicate. The reaction was immediate and explosive. The news of Hayes' corruption and her ties to the Syndicate dominated the headlines, sparking outrage and calls for her resignation and prosecution.

As the public outcry grew, Hayes attempted to defend herself, but the evidence was overwhelming. The media coverage was relentless, and her political allies began to distance themselves, fearing the backlash. The government launched an official investigation, and Hayes was placed under intense scrutiny.

Amidst the chaos, Alex and Sarah continued to operate from the shadows, monitoring the situation and preparing for their next move. They knew that exposing Hayes was only the first step. The real challenge would be to take her down without compromising their own safety.

As they planned the operation, they received an unexpected message from The Handler. The screen flickered to life, displaying the familiar cryptic message:

"Well done, Alex. Exposing Hayes has weakened the Syndicate's political influence. Your next task is to eliminate her. Her removal will destabilize the Syndicate further and create an opportunity to dismantle their remaining operations. Stay vigilant."

Alex showed the message to Sarah, his expression grim. "The Handler wants us to take out Hayes. This will be our most dangerous mission yet."

Sarah nodded, her eyes reflecting a mixture of determination and concern. "We need to be careful. Hayes is heavily guarded, and any misstep could expose us. But if we succeed, it will cripple the Syndicate's political operations."

They spent the next few days finalizing their plan. Hayes was under constant surveillance and surrounded by security, making it difficult to get close to her. They decided to strike during a public appearance she was scheduled to make at a charity gala. The event would provide the cover they needed to execute the mission without drawing immediate suspicion.

On the night of the gala, Alex and Sarah arrived at the venue, using their network of contacts to gain access. They blended in with the other guests, their formal attire and composed demeanor masking their true intentions. The gala was a lavish affair, attended by the city's elite, and security was tight.

As Hayes took the stage to give her speech, Alex positioned himself strategically, waiting for the right moment to strike. Sarah monitored the situation from a safe distance, ready to provide support if needed. The tension in the air was palpable as they waited for their opportunity.

Hayes began her speech, her voice confident and composed. She spoke about her commitment to the community and her dedication to public service, her words laced with hypocrisy given what Alex and Sarah knew about her true nature. As she spoke, Alex moved closer, his silenced pistol concealed beneath his jacket.

The moment came when Hayes paused to take a sip of water. Alex moved swiftly, drawing his weapon and taking aim. The shot was fired with precision, the sound barely audible over the applause and chatter of the audience. Hayes' body jerked, and she collapsed to the ground, the glass slipping from her hand.

For a moment, there was stunned silence, followed by chaos as the crowd realized what had happened. Security personnel rushed to the stage, and the guests scrambled for the exits. Amidst the confusion, Alex and Sarah made their way to the exit, using the chaos to cover their escape.

They drove away from the venue, their hearts pounding with adrenaline and relief. The mission had been a success, but they knew that the repercussions would be significant. The assassination of Senator Hayes would send shockwaves through the Syndicate and the political landscape of Veridan.

Back at their hideout, they reviewed the aftermath of the operation. The news of Hayes' assassination dominated the headlines, sparking even more outrage and calls for justice. The government intensified its investigation into the Syndicate, launching raids and arresting key figures associated with the organization.

The public's reaction was one of shock and anger. Hayes had been a prominent political figure, and her death highlighted the extent of the Syndicate's corruption and influence. The government faced increasing pressure to dismantle the organization and restore public trust.

As Alex and Sarah watched the news coverage, they received another message from The Handler. The screen flickered to life, displaying the final and most dangerous task yet:

"Alex, you have done well. The Syndicate is weakened, but the battle is not over. Your final target is The Handler. They have been manipulating events from behind the scenes, and their removal is crucial to ensuring the Syndicate's downfall. Be prepared. This will be your most challenging mission yet. Stay vigilant."

Alex stared at the message, his mind racing with questions. The Handler had guided him through every mission, providing information and instructions, but their true identity and motives had always been a mystery. Now, he was being tasked with eliminating the very person who had orchestrated his actions.

Sarah read the message over his shoulder, her expression one of determination. "This is it, Alex. We need to find out who The Handler is and stop them once and for all. But we need to be careful. This could be a trap."

Alex nodded, his resolve firm. "I know. But we have to do this. The Syndicate won't truly be defeated until we take down The Handler. We need to gather as much information as we can and plan our next move."

Over the next few days, Alex and Sarah focused on uncovering The Handler's true identity. They analyzed the communications they had received, tracing the origins and looking for any clues that could lead them to the source. It was a complex and challenging task, but they were determined to find answers.

Their investigation led them to discover a series of encrypted messages and coded communications that pointed to a high-ranking government official with deep connections to the Syndicate. The clues were sparse, but they began to piece together a profile of The Handler, narrowing down the list of suspects.

As they delved deeper, they uncovered evidence that suggested The Handler was using their position within the government to manipulate events and protect the Syndicate's interests. The realization that The Handler was someone within the very system they were trying to protect was a sobering one.

One evening, as they reviewed their findings, Sarah received a tip from one of her trusted sources. The tip indicated that The Handler would be attending a secret meeting with the Syndicate's remaining leaders to discuss their next steps. The meeting was set to take place at a secure location in the heart of the city.

Alex and Sarah knew that this was their chance to uncover The Handler's identity and put an end to their manipulation. They began to formulate a plan to infiltrate the meeting and gather the evidence they needed to expose The Handler.

The location of the meeting was a luxurious penthouse in one of Veridan's most exclusive neighborhoods. The building had state-of-the-art security, including biometric access controls, surveillance cameras, and armed guards. Alex and Sarah knew that gaining access would be challenging, but they were determined to succeed.

On the night of the meeting, Alex and Sarah arrived at the building, using disguises to blend in with the staff and guests. Alex had obtained a stolen access card from a contact, which allowed them to bypass the initial security checkpoint. They took the elevator to the top floor, their hearts pounding with anticipation.

As they approached the penthouse, Alex used a device to hack into the building's security system, temporarily disabling the cameras and alarms. They moved quickly and silently, reaching the door to the penthouse without being detected. Alex picked the lock with practiced ease, and they slipped inside.

The penthouse was lavishly decorated, with floor-to-ceiling windows offering stunning views of the city. In the center of the living room, a group of well-dressed individuals sat around a large table, deep in discussion. Alex and Sarah recognized several of them as key figures within the Syndicate, including their current target, The Handler.

Alex set up a small camera to record the meeting, positioning it discreetly behind a decorative sculpture. He and Sarah then took up positions where they could listen and observe without being seen. The leaders of the Syndicate were discussing their plans to recover from the recent setbacks, including strategies to protect their remaining assets and counter the actions of Alex and Sarah.

The conversation revealed the full extent of The Syndicate's influence and their willingness to use any means necessary to achieve their goals. They discussed bribing officials, manipulating media coverage, and even resorting to violence to maintain control. It was clear that The Syndicate was a formidable and ruthless organization, willing to go to any lengths to protect their power.

As the meeting continued, Alex and Sarah's presence was suddenly detected. One of the security guards had noticed the disabled cameras and raised the alarm. The leaders of The Syndicate reacted quickly, ordering their guards to secure the penthouse and find the intruders.

Alex and Sarah knew they had to act fast. They retrieved the camera and made their way to the nearest exit, but they were confronted by armed guards. A fierce firefight ensued, with Alex and Sarah using their training and skills to fight their way out. Bullets flew, and the sounds of gunfire echoed through the penthouse.

Despite the overwhelming odds, Alex and Sarah managed to escape, but not without injuries. They made their way to a safe house, where they treated their wounds and reviewed the footage they had captured. The evidence was damning, providing clear proof of The Syndicate's activities and their plans to manipulate political events.

With the footage in hand, Alex and Sarah contacted their allies in the media and law enforcement, arranging for a coordinated release of the information. The story broke the next day, sending shockwaves through Veridan and beyond. The public was stunned by the revelations, and calls for accountability grew louder.

The government launched a comprehensive investigation into The Syndicate, resulting in the arrest of several key figures and the seizure of their assets. The organization's influence began to wane, and their grip on Veridan weakened. The successful operation had dealt a significant blow to The Syndicate, but Alex and Sarah knew that their work was far from over.

As the city continued to grapple with the fallout from the revelations, Alex and Sarah remained focused on their mission. They had exposed the puppet masters who had been manipulating political events, but they knew that there were still threats to be eliminated and secrets to be uncovered.

The battle against The Syndicate was not yet won, but Alex and Sarah were ready to face whatever challenges lay ahead. Their resolve was stronger than ever, and they were determined to continue fighting for justice and a future free from corruption and control. As they looked out over the city, they felt a renewed sense of purpose, knowing that the pursuit of justice was a journey that never truly ended.

Chapter 13: The Final Target

The city of Veridan had become a battleground for truth and justice, and Alex Morgan and Sarah Mitchell were at the center of the storm. They had exposed the Syndicate's corruption, disrupted their operations, and brought key figures to justice. But their mission was not complete. The most elusive and dangerous target remained: The Handler, the puppet master who had orchestrated the Syndicate's actions from the shadows.

For weeks, Alex and Sarah had been piecing together clues about The Handler's true identity. Their investigation led them to discover a high-ranking government official who had used his position to manipulate events and protect the Syndicate's interests. The realization that The Handler was someone within the very system they were trying to protect was both sobering and infuriating.

One evening, as they reviewed their findings, Sarah turned to Alex with a determined expression. "We've identified The Handler. It's Senator Charles Donovan. He's been using his influence to shield the Syndicate and direct their operations. We need to take him down."

Alex nodded, his expression grim. "Donovan is powerful and well-protected. This will be our most challenging mission yet. But we need to expose his true nature and stop him once and for all."

They spent the next few days gathering evidence and finalizing their plan. They knew that Donovan would be attending a high-profile political event in the heart of Veridan's capital, a perfect opportunity to confront him and expose his crimes. The event was heavily guarded, and the stakes were high, but Alex and Sarah were determined to succeed.

On the night of the event, Alex and Sarah arrived at the venue, using their network of contacts to gain access. Dressed in formal attire, they blended in with the other guests, their composed demeanor masking the tension and anticipation they felt. The grand hall was filled with politicians, business leaders, and influential figures, all unaware of the danger in their midst.

As they moved through the crowd, Alex kept a close eye on Donovan, who was mingling with guests and exuding confidence and charm. Donovan was a skilled politician, his public persona hiding his true nature as the mastermind behind the Syndicate's operations.

Sarah, meanwhile, positioned herself strategically, ready to record the confrontation and ensure that the evidence would be widely disseminated. They had coordinated their plan meticulously, knowing that timing and precision were crucial.

The moment came when Donovan took the stage to give a speech. Alex moved closer, his heart pounding with anticipation. As Donovan began to speak, Alex interrupted, his voice cutting through the applause and chatter.

"Senator Donovan, your time is up."

The crowd fell silent, turning to see Alex standing with a determined expression. Donovan's eyes widened in surprise, but he quickly composed himself, a cold smile playing on his lips.

"Mr. Morgan, what is the meaning of this?" Donovan asked, his voice steady but laced with menace.

Alex stepped forward, his voice firm. "The meaning is simple. You've been manipulating events from behind the scenes, using your position to protect the Syndicate and orchestrate their crimes. The people of Veridan deserve to know the truth."

Donovan's smile faded, replaced by a look of cold fury. "You're making a grave mistake, Mr. Morgan. You have no idea who you're dealing with."

Sarah stepped forward, holding up a device that projected the evidence they had gathered onto a large screen. The crowd gasped as they saw the damning documents, emails, and recordings that detailed Donovan's involvement with the Syndicate.

"This is who you're dealing with, Senator," Sarah said, her voice steady. "The evidence is irrefutable. Your crimes are exposed for all to see."

The room erupted in chaos as guests began to react to the shocking revelations. Security personnel rushed to the stage, but Alex and Sarah were prepared. They moved quickly, using the confusion to their advantage.

A fierce confrontation ensued, with Donovan's guards attempting to protect him and Alex and Sarah fighting to bring him to justice. Bullets flew, and the sounds of gunfire echoed through the grand hall. The stakes were higher than ever, and the outcome was uncertain.

Despite the overwhelming odds, Alex and Sarah fought with determination and skill. They managed to incapacitate Donovan's guards, but the battle had taken its toll. They were both injured, but their resolve remained unbroken.

As Donovan attempted to flee, Alex pursued him, determined to end this once and for all. They reached a secluded corridor, and Donovan turned to face Alex, a look of desperation in his eyes.

"This isn't over, Morgan," Donovan spat, his voice filled with venom. "You'll never stop the Syndicate. They'll come for you."

Alex raised his weapon, his voice steady. "It ends here, Donovan. Your reign of terror is over."

With a final, decisive move, Alex fired, the shot echoing through the corridor. Donovan fell to the ground, his life extinguished. The battle was over, but the cost had been high.

Alex made his way back to the grand hall, where Sarah was waiting. She had managed to secure the evidence and ensure that it was being transmitted to the media and authorities. The news of Donovan's corruption and his role as The Handler spread quickly, sparking outrage and calls for justice.

As the government launched a comprehensive investigation, Alex and Sarah reflected on their journey. They had faced incredible odds, but their determination and partnership had prevailed. The Syndicate was dismantled, and its leaders brought to justice. The city of Veridan could finally begin to heal.

But as they stood together, Alex couldn't shake the feeling that the battle had taken a toll on his soul. He had faced his own demons, confronted the moral cost of his actions, and emerged stronger. But the journey had changed him in ways he couldn't fully comprehend.

Sarah, sensing his turmoil, placed a hand on his shoulder. "We did it, Alex. We brought them to justice. But I know this hasn't been easy for you."

Alex nodded, his expression somber. "I've done things I'm not proud of, Sarah. But I believe it was necessary to stop them. I just hope that in the end, it was worth it."

Sarah smiled, her eyes filled with understanding. "It was worth it, Alex. You've made a difference, and the people of Veridan will remember that. We've exposed the corruption, and now it's up to the people to rebuild and create a better future."

As they looked out over the city, Alex and Sarah felt a renewed sense of purpose. The battle against the Syndicate was over, but the fight for justice and truth would continue. They knew that the pursuit of justice was a journey that never truly ended, but they were ready to face whatever challenges lay ahead.

Together, they had faced the darkness and emerged stronger. And they knew that as long as they stood together, they could overcome any obstacle and continue to fight for a brighter future.

The high-stakes confrontation in the heart of Veridan's capital had been the ultimate test of their resolve and partnership. They had exposed The Handler, brought him to justice, and dismantled the Syndicate's operations. The city of Veridan could now begin to heal and rebuild, free from the shadow of corruption and manipulation.

As the weeks passed, the government's investigation into the Syndicate continued, resulting in more arrests and the seizure of assets. The public's faith in the system was gradually being restored, and reforms were being implemented to prevent such corruption from taking hold again.

Alex and Sarah remained vigilant, knowing that their work was far from over. They continued to gather information, expose corruption, and support efforts to rebuild Veridan's institutions. Their alliance had become a powerful force for change, and their commitment to justice remained unwavering.

One evening, as they reviewed the latest developments, Alex received an unexpected message on his secure line. It was from a new source, someone claiming to have information about remnants of the Syndicate still operating in the shadows. The message was cryptic, but it hinted at a new threat that needed to be addressed.

Alex showed the message to Sarah, his expression serious. "It seems our work isn't done yet. There are still remnants of the Syndicate out there, and they're planning something."

Sarah nodded, her eyes reflecting determination. "We need to investigate this. We can't let the Syndicate regain its foothold. We've come too far to let that happen."

As they began to plan their next steps, Alex couldn't help but reflect on the journey that had brought them to this point. They had faced incredible challenges, made difficult choices, and confronted their own fears and doubts. But through it all, they had remained true to their mission and to each other.

Their partnership had been forged in the crucible of conflict, and it had become a powerful force for justice. They knew that the road ahead would be filled with new challenges and threats, but they were ready to face them together.

As they prepared to embark on their next mission, Alex felt a renewed sense of purpose. The battle against the Syndicate had been a defining chapter in their lives, but it was not the end. The pursuit of justice was a journey that never truly ended, and they were ready to continue that journey, no matter where it led.

Together, they would face the darkness and fight for a brighter future. They had overcome incredible odds, and they knew that as long as they stood together, they could overcome any obstacle and continue to make a difference in the world.

The battle for Veridan's soul had been won, but the fight for justice and truth would continue. And Alex and Sarah were ready to face whatever challenges lay ahead, driven by their shared commitment to making the world a better place.

Chapter 14: The Reckoning

The city of Veridan was finally beginning to breathe again. The Syndicate, a shadowy organization that had manipulated and controlled the political landscape for years, was crumbling. With the downfall of The Handler, the puppet master who had orchestrated the Syndicate's nefarious activities, the organization's collapse was imminent. But for Alex Morgan and Sarah Mitchell, the journey was far from over. The reckoning was at hand, and the consequences of their actions were about to unfold.

The news of Senator Charles Donovan's true identity as The Handler and his subsequent death had sent shockwaves through the city. The media was abuzz with coverage, and the public was demanding accountability and justice. The government, under immense pressure, had launched a comprehensive investigation into the Syndicate, leading to numerous arrests and the seizure of assets. The political landscape of Veridan was beginning to stabilize, but the scars of corruption and manipulation ran deep.

Alex and Sarah watched from the sidelines as the government's efforts to dismantle the Syndicate gained momentum. They had played a pivotal role in exposing the truth, but they knew that their work was not yet complete. There were still remnants of the Syndicate operating in the shadows, and the fight for justice and transparency was far from over.

One evening, as they sat in their safe house, Alex reflected on the journey that had brought them to this point. He had been a lone wolf, a former military operative turned assassin, driven by a desire to fight against corruption and injustice. But the path he had chosen was fraught with moral ambiguity, and the consequences of his actions weighed heavily on his mind.

Sarah, sensing his turmoil, placed a hand on his arm. "Alex, you've done so much to bring down the Syndicate and expose the truth. But I know this hasn't been easy for you. You've faced incredible challenges and made difficult choices."

Alex nodded, his expression somber. "I've killed people, Sarah. Some of them were deeply corrupt, but others... I can't help but question the morality of my actions. Did I cross a line? Was there another way?"

Sarah's eyes were filled with understanding. "We've both made sacrifices, Alex. And we've both done things we're not proud of. But we did what we believed was necessary to bring about change. You've made a difference, and now it's time to confront the consequences and find a way forward."

As they continued to talk, Alex realized that he needed to come to terms with his actions and the impact they had on his soul. He had been driven by a desire for justice, but the path he had taken was one of violence and retribution. He needed to find a way to reconcile his past and move forward with a renewed sense of purpose.

Meanwhile, Sarah's exposé on the Syndicate had gained significant traction. Her relentless pursuit of the truth had brought the organization's corruption and manipulation to light, and her work was sparking a movement for transparency and justice. The public was rallying behind her, demanding reforms and accountability from the government.

Sarah's dedication to her mission was unwavering. She continued to uncover new evidence, expose corrupt officials, and hold those in power accountable. Her work was bringing hope to the people of Veridan, inspiring a new era of transparency and justice.

As the government's investigation into the Syndicate progressed, the political landscape of Veridan began to stabilize. Reforms were being implemented to prevent such corruption from taking hold again, and new leaders were emerging with a commitment to integrity and accountability.

One day, as Alex and Sarah reviewed the latest developments, they received an unexpected visitor. It was Senator Emily Carter, a staunch ally in their fight against the Syndicate. She had been following their journey closely and had come to offer her support and gratitude.

"Alex, Sarah, you've done an incredible job exposing the Syndicate and bringing its leaders to justice," Senator Carter said, her voice filled with admiration. "Your work has paved the way for a new era in Veridan, one where transparency and justice can prevail."

Alex nodded, his expression thoughtful. "We've made progress, Senator, but there's still much to be done. The Syndicate's remnants are still out there, and we need to ensure that they don't regain their foothold."

Senator Carter smiled. "I understand, Alex. And that's why I'm here. The government is committed to continuing the fight against corruption and ensuring that the reforms we're implementing are effective. But we need people like you and Sarah to keep pushing for change, to keep holding those in power accountable."

Sarah's eyes lit up with determination. "We're not done yet, Senator. We'll continue to uncover the truth and expose corruption wherever it exists. The people of Veridan deserve nothing less."

As Senator Carter left, Alex and Sarah felt a renewed sense of purpose. They had come a long way, but the fight for justice and transparency was far from over. They knew that their work would be challenging, but they were ready to face whatever obstacles lay ahead.

The following weeks were marked by significant progress in the government's investigation into the Syndicate. Key figures were arrested, assets were seized, and new evidence continued to emerge, providing a clearer picture of the organization's operations and connections.

Sarah's exposé had become a catalyst for change, inspiring a movement for transparency and accountability. Her work was being recognized not just in Veridan, but beyond, as a shining example of the power of journalism and the importance of holding those in power accountable.

One evening, as Alex and Sarah reviewed the latest developments, Alex received a message on his secure line. It was from a new source, someone claiming to have information about the remaining Syndicate operatives. The message was cryptic, but it hinted at a new threat that needed to be addressed.

Alex showed the message to Sarah, his expression serious. "It seems our work isn't done yet. There are still remnants of the Syndicate out there, and they're planning something."

Sarah nodded, her eyes reflecting determination. "We need to investigate this. We can't let the Syndicate regain its foothold. We've come too far to let that happen."

As they began to plan their next steps, Alex couldn't help but reflect on the journey that had brought them to this point. They had faced incredible challenges, made difficult choices, and confronted their own fears and doubts. But through it all, they had remained true to their mission and to each other.

Their partnership had been forged in the crucible of conflict, and it had become a powerful force for change. They knew that the road ahead would be filled with new challenges and threats, but they were ready to face them together.

As they prepared to embark on their next mission, Alex felt a renewed sense of purpose. The battle against the Syndicate had been a defining chapter in their lives, but it was not the end. The pursuit of justice was a journey that never truly ended, and they were ready to continue that journey, no matter where it led.

Together, they would face the darkness and fight for a brighter future. They had overcome incredible odds, and they knew that as long as they stood together, they could overcome any obstacle and continue to make a difference in the world.

The battle for Veridan's soul had been won, but the fight for justice and truth would continue. And Alex and Sarah were ready to face whatever challenges lay ahead, driven by their shared commitment to making the world a better place.

As the weeks passed, Alex and Sarah continued to gather intelligence and uncover new threats. They worked closely with Senator Carter and other allies to ensure that the reforms being implemented were effective and that the remnants of the Syndicate were rooted out.

One evening, as they reviewed their findings, they received a message from one of their trusted sources. The message indicated that a high-ranking member of the Syndicate's remnants was planning a major operation to destabilize the government and regain control.

Alex and Sarah knew that they needed to act quickly. They began to formulate a plan to intercept the operation and bring the remaining Syndicate operatives to justice. The stakes were high, and the outcome was uncertain, but they were determined to succeed.

On the night of the operation, Alex and Sarah moved swiftly and decisively. They infiltrated the Syndicate's hideout, using their skills and training to navigate the complex and avoid detection. As they approached the main control room, they overheard the operatives discussing their plans to disrupt the government and create chaos.

Alex and Sarah moved in, their weapons at the ready. A fierce confrontation ensued, with bullets flying and the sounds of gunfire echoing through the hideout. Despite the overwhelming odds, they fought with determination and skill, determined to stop the Syndicate's plans.

As the dust settled, Alex and Sarah stood victorious. The remaining Syndicate operatives had been apprehended, and their plans had been thwarted. The operation had been a success, but the cost had been high. They were both injured, but their resolve remained unbroken.

Back at their safe house, they reviewed the evidence they had gathered. The information provided further insights into the Syndicate's operations and their plans to manipulate political events. They compiled the information into a comprehensive report, ready to be disseminated to the media and law enforcement.

The following day, the story broke, sending shockwaves through Veridan and beyond. The public was stunned by the revelations, and calls for accountability grew louder. The government launched a comprehensive investigation into the Syndicate, resulting in the arrest of several key figures and the seizure of their assets. The organization's influence began to wane, and their grip on Veridan weakened.

As the city continued to grapple with the fallout from the revelations, Alex and Sarah remained focused on their mission. They had exposed the puppet masters who had been manipulating political events, but they knew that there were still threats to be eliminated and secrets to be uncovered.

The battle against the Syndicate was not yet won, but Alex and Sarah were ready to face whatever challenges lay ahead. Their resolve was stronger than ever, and they were determined to continue fighting for justice and a future free from corruption and control. As they looked out over the city, they felt a renewed sense of purpose, knowing that the pursuit of justice was a journey that never truly ended.

In the weeks that followed, Alex and Sarah continued to work tirelessly to ensure that the Syndicate's influence was completely eradicated. Their efforts paid off, as more operatives were arrested and their operations dismantled. The political landscape of Veridan began to stabilize, and new leaders emerged with a commitment to integrity and transparency.

Sarah's exposé had become a beacon of hope for the people of Veridan. Her work had inspired a movement for transparency and justice, and her dedication to uncovering the truth was recognized and celebrated. The public rallied behind her, demanding reforms and accountability from their leaders.

One evening, as Alex and Sarah reflected on their journey, Alex couldn't help but feel a sense of pride in what they had accomplished. They had faced incredible challenges and made difficult choices, but their determination and partnership had prevailed. They had brought down the Syndicate, exposed corruption, and helped pave the way for a new era in Veridan.

But Alex also knew that the battle had taken a toll on him. He had been driven by a desire for justice, but the path he had taken was one of violence and retribution. He needed to come to terms with his actions and find a way to move forward with a renewed sense of purpose.

Sarah, sensing his turmoil, placed a hand on his shoulder. "You've made a difference, Alex. You've helped bring about change and expose the truth. But I know this hasn't been easy for you. You've faced your own demons and the moral cost of your actions."

Alex nodded, his expression somber. "I've done things I'm not proud of, Sarah. But I believe it was necessary to stop them. I just hope that in the end, it was worth it."

Sarah smiled, her eyes filled with understanding. "It was worth it, Alex. You've made a difference, and the people of Veridan will remember that. We've exposed the corruption, and now it's up to the people to rebuild and create a better future."

As they looked out over the city, Alex and Sarah felt a renewed sense of purpose. The battle against the Syndicate had been a defining chapter in their lives, but it was not the end. The pursuit of justice was a journey that never truly ended, and they were ready to continue that journey, no matter where it led.

Together, they would face the darkness and fight for a brighter future. They had overcome incredible odds, and they knew that as long as they stood together, they could overcome any obstacle and continue to make a difference in the world.

The battle for Veridan's soul had been won, but the fight for justice and truth would continue. And Alex and Sarah were ready to face whatever challenges lay ahead, driven by their shared commitment to making the world a better place.

The city of Veridan was beginning to heal, and the people were starting to believe in the possibility of a brighter future. The Syndicate's reign of terror had been brought to an end, and the public's faith in the system was gradually being restored. Reforms were being implemented, and new leaders were emerging with a commitment to integrity and accountability.

But the journey was not over for Alex and Sarah. They knew that the fight for justice and transparency was a never-ending battle, and they were ready to continue that fight. Their partnership had become a powerful force for change, and they were determined to keep pushing forward, no matter the obstacles.

As they prepared to embark on their next mission, Alex felt a renewed sense of purpose. The battle against the Syndicate had been a defining chapter in their lives, but it was not the end. The pursuit of justice was a journey that never truly ended, and they were ready to continue that journey, no matter where it led.

Together, they would face the darkness and fight for a brighter future. They had overcome incredible odds, and they knew that as long as they stood together, they could overcome any obstacle and continue to make a difference in the world.

The battle for Veridan's soul had been won, but the fight for justice and truth would continue. And Alex and Sarah were ready to face whatever challenges lay ahead, driven by their shared commitment to making the world a better place.

Chapter 15: A New Dawn

The city of Veridan was awakening to a new reality. The Syndicate, which had cast a long shadow over the city's politics and economy, was no more. Its leaders were either dead or imprisoned, its operations dismantled, and its assets seized. The public, once disillusioned and apathetic, now had hope for a brighter future. The hard-fought battle for justice had been won, but for Alex Morgan and Sarah Mitchell, the journey was far from over.

Alex stood on the balcony of their safe house, gazing out over the city. The dawn was breaking, casting a warm glow over the skyline. It was a sight that should have filled him with hope and a sense of accomplishment, but instead, he felt a deep sense of conflict. The end of the Syndicate had brought him to a crossroads, forcing him to confront his past and decide his future.

As he stood lost in thought, Sarah joined him on the balcony, her presence a comforting reminder of their shared mission. She had been his anchor, guiding him through the darkest moments and helping him find a path forward. Together, they had faced incredible odds and emerged victorious, but now, Alex was unsure of what came next.

"Penny for your thoughts?" Sarah asked, her voice gentle.

Alex sighed, his gaze still fixed on the horizon. "I've been thinking about everything we've been through, the choices I've made, and the people I've hurt. I can't help but wonder if there's any redemption for someone like me."

Sarah placed a hand on his arm, her touch grounding him. "You've done a lot of good, Alex. You've helped bring down a corrupt organization and exposed the truth. That counts for something. But I understand that it's not that simple."

Alex turned to face her, his eyes filled with turmoil. "I've killed people, Sarah. Some of them were deeply corrupt, but others were caught in the crossfire. I chose a path of violence and retribution, and I'm not sure if I can ever make up for that."

Sarah's eyes were filled with understanding and compassion. "You did what you believed was necessary to stop the Syndicate. But now, you have a chance to choose a different path. You can use your skills and experience to help rebuild and create something better."

Alex nodded, taking in her words. "I want to believe that. But I also need to find a way to come to terms with my past. I can't move forward until I've faced my demons."

Sarah squeezed his arm reassuringly. "You don't have to do it alone, Alex. We've been through so much together, and we'll continue to face whatever comes our way. The fight for justice and truth isn't over, but we can face it together."

As they stood together, the sun continued to rise, casting a warm glow over the city. It was a new dawn, a symbol of hope and the possibility of change. For Alex, it was also a reminder that redemption was a journey, one that required courage, introspection, and a willingness to change.

The aftermath of the Syndicate's demise was being felt across Veridan's political landscape. The government's investigation had led to significant arrests and the seizure of assets, but it had also exposed the deep-rooted corruption that had allowed the Syndicate to thrive. New leaders were emerging, committed to integrity and transparency, but the path to true reform was fraught with challenges.

Senator Emily Carter, one of their staunchest allies, was at the forefront of the reform movement. She had been instrumental in pushing for accountability and transparency, and her efforts were beginning to bear fruit. The public's faith in the system was gradually being restored, and there was a renewed sense of optimism about the future.

Sarah, meanwhile, continued her relentless pursuit of the truth. Her exposé on the Syndicate had brought her widespread recognition and acclaim, but she remained focused on her mission. She was determined to continue uncovering corruption and holding those in power accountable, and her work was inspiring a new generation of journalists and activists.

One day, as Alex and Sarah were discussing their next steps, they received an invitation from Senator Carter to attend a public forum on government reform. The event was designed to engage the public and gather input on the proposed reforms, and Carter believed that Alex and Sarah's presence would lend credibility and momentum to the cause.

Alex was hesitant at first, unsure if he was ready to step into the spotlight and face the public. But Sarah encouraged him, reminding him of the impact their work had already had and the importance of continuing to push for change.

The forum was held in a large auditorium, filled with citizens eager to participate in the discussion. Senator Carter opened the event with a passionate speech about the need for accountability and transparency, and the importance of public engagement in the reform process.

As the forum progressed, Sarah was invited to speak about her work and the role of journalism in exposing corruption. She spoke eloquently and passionately, highlighting the power of the press in holding those in power accountable and the importance of a free and independent media.

When it was Alex's turn to speak, he felt a surge of nervousness and uncertainty. But as he looked out at the audience, he saw the faces of people who had been affected by the Syndicate's corruption and manipulation. He took a deep breath and began to speak from the heart.

"I'm not a politician or a journalist. I'm a man who has made a lot of mistakes and taken a path that has caused a lot of pain. But I believe in the power of redemption and the possibility of change. We've all seen the damage that corruption can do, and we've all felt the effects of a system that prioritizes power and profit over people."

He paused, gathering his thoughts. "But we also have the power to change that. We can demand accountability, we can push for transparency, and we can hold our leaders to a higher standard. It won't be easy, and it won't happen overnight, but together, we can create a better future for Veridan."

The audience erupted in applause, and Alex felt a sense of relief and validation. He had faced his fears and spoken his truth, and the response was overwhelmingly positive. It was a small step, but it was a step forward, and it gave him hope for the future.

As the forum concluded, Alex and Sarah were approached by numerous citizens and activists, eager to share their stories and offer their support. It was a powerful reminder of the impact their work had had and the importance of continuing to fight for justice and transparency.

In the weeks that followed, Alex and Sarah continued to work tirelessly to ensure that the reforms being implemented were effective and that the remnants of the Syndicate were rooted out. Their efforts were paying off, as more operatives were arrested and their operations dismantled. The political landscape of Veridan was beginning to stabilize, and new leaders were emerging with a commitment to integrity and accountability.

Sarah's exposé had become a beacon of hope for the people of Veridan. Her work had inspired a movement for transparency and justice, and her dedication to uncovering the truth was recognized and celebrated. The public rallied behind her, demanding reforms and accountability from their leaders.

One evening, as Alex and Sarah reflected on their journey, Alex couldn't help but feel a sense of pride in what they had accomplished. They had faced incredible challenges and made difficult choices, but their determination and partnership had prevailed. They had brought down the Syndicate, exposed corruption, and helped pave the way for a new era in Veridan.

But Alex also knew that the battle had taken a toll on him. He had been driven by a desire for justice, but the path he had taken was one of violence and retribution. He needed to come to terms with his actions and find a way to move forward with a renewed sense of purpose.

Sarah, sensing his turmoil, placed a hand on his shoulder. "You've made a difference, Alex. You've helped bring about change and expose the truth. But I know this hasn't been easy for you. You've faced your own demons and the moral cost of your actions."

Alex nodded, his expression somber. "I've done things I'm not proud of, Sarah. But I believe it was necessary to stop them. I just hope that in the end, it was worth it."

Sarah smiled, her eyes filled with understanding. "It was worth it, Alex. You've made a difference, and the people of Veridan will remember that. We've exposed the corruption, and now it's up to the people to rebuild and create a better future."

As they looked out over the city, Alex and Sarah felt a renewed sense of purpose. The battle against the Syndicate had been a defining chapter in their lives, but it was not the end. The pursuit of justice was a journey that never truly ended, and they were ready to continue that journey, no matter where it led.

Together, they would face the darkness and fight for a brighter future. They had overcome incredible odds, and they knew that as long as they stood together, they could overcome any obstacle and continue to make a difference in the world.

The battle for Veridan's soul had been won, but the fight for justice and truth would continue. And Alex and Sarah were ready to face whatever challenges lay ahead, driven by their shared commitment to making the world a better place.

As the city of Veridan continued to heal, Alex and Sarah's work began to take on new dimensions. They were no longer just fighting against corruption; they were actively working to build a better future. They collaborated with community leaders, activists, and policymakers to develop and implement reforms that would ensure transparency and accountability in government.

Sarah's journalism continued to play a crucial role in this process. Her investigative reporting uncovered new stories of corruption and injustice, keeping the public informed and engaged. Her work was widely recognized and celebrated, and she became a leading voice in the movement for transparency and accountability.

Alex, meanwhile, found new ways to use his skills for the greater good. He began to work with community organizations, helping to develop security protocols and training programs that would protect vulnerable populations from exploitation and abuse. He also became a mentor to young activists and advocates, sharing his experiences and guiding them on their own paths to making a difference.

One day, as they were reviewing the latest developments, they received a call from Senator Emily Carter. She had some important news to share and invited them to her office for a meeting.

When they arrived, Senator Carter greeted them warmly and led them to a conference room. "Alex, Sarah, I wanted to thank you both personally for everything you've done. Your efforts have been instrumental in bringing about real change in Veridan. I have some news that I think you'll find encouraging."

She handed them a report outlining the progress that had been made in implementing the reforms they had fought for. The report detailed the new measures that had been put in place to ensure transparency and accountability, as well as the positive impact these changes were already having on the city.

"I'm pleased to report that the reforms are working," Senator Carter said, her voice filled with pride. "We've seen a significant decrease in corruption and an increase in public trust in government. The people of Veridan are beginning to believe in the possibility of a brighter future."

Alex and Sarah exchanged a glance, feeling a sense of accomplishment and relief. Their efforts had not been in vain, and the city was beginning to heal.

Senator Carter continued, "I also wanted to let you know that we're planning a public event to celebrate the progress we've made and to honor those who have played a key role in this movement. We would be honored if you both would attend and speak about your experiences and the importance of continuing this fight."

Alex felt a surge of nervousness at the thought of speaking in public again, but Sarah squeezed his hand reassuringly. "We'd be honored, Senator. Thank you."

As they left the senator's office, Alex felt a renewed sense of purpose. The journey they had been on had been long and difficult, but it had led to real change. He was beginning to see the possibility of redemption and a brighter future, not just for Veridan, but for himself as well.

The day of the event arrived, and the public square was filled with citizens eager to celebrate the progress that had been made. The atmosphere was one of hope and optimism, a stark contrast to the fear and uncertainty that had gripped the city during the Syndicate's reign.

Senator Carter opened the event with a passionate speech about the importance of transparency and accountability, and the power of the people to bring about change. She spoke about the challenges they had faced and the progress that had been made, and she praised the efforts of those who had fought for justice and truth.

When it was Sarah's turn to speak, she took the stage with confidence and grace. She spoke about her work as a journalist, the importance of uncovering the truth, and the power of the press in holding those in power accountable. Her words were met with enthusiastic applause, a testament to the impact she had made.

Then it was Alex's turn. As he stepped up to the podium, he felt a mixture of nervousness and determination. He took a deep breath and began to speak from the heart.

"I'm not a politician or a journalist. I'm a man who has made a lot of mistakes and taken a path that has caused a lot of pain. But I believe in the power of redemption and the possibility of change. We've all seen the damage that corruption can do, and we've all felt the effects of a system that prioritizes power and profit over people."

He paused, gathering his thoughts. "But we also have the power to change that. We can demand accountability, we can push for transparency, and we can hold our leaders to a higher standard. It won't be easy, and it won't happen overnight, but together, we can create a better future for Veridan."

The audience erupted in applause, and Alex felt a sense of relief and validation. He had faced his fears and spoken his truth, and the response was overwhelmingly positive. It was a small step, but it was a step forward, and it gave him hope for the future.

As the event concluded, Alex and Sarah were approached by numerous citizens and activists, eager to share their stories and offer their support. It was a powerful reminder of the impact their work had had and the importance of continuing to fight for justice and transparency.

In the days that followed, Alex and Sarah continued to work tirelessly to ensure that the reforms being implemented were effective and that the remnants of the Syndicate were rooted out. Their efforts were paying off, as more operatives were arrested and their operations dismantled. The political landscape of Veridan was beginning to stabilize, and new leaders were emerging with a commitment to integrity and accountability.

Sarah's exposé had become a beacon of hope for the people of Veridan. Her work had inspired a movement for transparency and justice, and her dedication to uncovering the truth was recognized and celebrated. The public rallied behind her, demanding reforms and accountability from their leaders.

One evening, as Alex and Sarah reflected on their journey, Alex couldn't help but feel a sense of pride in what they had accomplished. They had faced incredible challenges and made difficult choices, but their determination and partnership had prevailed. They had brought down the Syndicate, exposed corruption, and helped pave the way for a new era in Veridan.

But Alex also knew that the battle had taken a toll on him. He had been driven by a desire for justice, but the path he had taken was one of violence and retribution. He needed to come to terms with his actions and find a way to move forward with a renewed sense of purpose.

Sarah, sensing his turmoil, placed a hand on his shoulder. "You've made a difference, Alex. You've helped bring about change and expose the truth. But I know this hasn't been easy for you. You've faced your own demons and the moral cost of your actions."

Alex nodded, his expression somber. "I've done things I'm not proud of, Sarah. But I believe it was necessary to stop them. I just hope that in the end, it was worth it."

Sarah smiled, her eyes filled with understanding. "It was worth it, Alex. You've made a difference, and the people of Veridan will remember that. We've exposed the corruption, and now it's up to the people to rebuild and create a better future."

As they looked out over the city, Alex and Sarah felt a renewed sense of purpose. The battle against the Syndicate had been a defining chapter in their lives, but it was not the end. The pursuit of justice was a journey that never truly ended, and they were ready to continue that journey, no matter where it led.

Together, they would face the darkness and fight for a brighter future. They had overcome incredible odds, and they knew that as long as they stood together, they could overcome any obstacle and continue to make a difference in the world.

The battle for Veridan's soul had been won, but the fight for justice and truth would continue. And Alex and Sarah were ready to face whatever challenges lay ahead, driven by their shared commitment to making the world a better place. The city of Veridan was beginning to heal, and the people were starting to believe in the possibility of a brighter future. The Syndicate's reign of terror had been brought to an end, and the public's faith in the system was gradually being restored. Reforms were being implemented, and new leaders were emerging with a commitment to integrity and accountability.

But the journey was not over for Alex and Sarah. They knew that the fight for justice and transparency was a never-ending battle, and they were ready to continue that fight. Their partnership had become a powerful force for change, and they were determined to keep pushing forward, no matter the obstacles.

As they prepared to embark on their next mission, Alex felt a renewed sense of purpose. The battle against the Syndicate had been a defining chapter in their lives, but it was not the end. The pursuit of justice was a journey that never truly ended, and they were ready to continue that journey, no matter where it led.

Together, they would face the darkness and fight for a brighter future. They had overcome incredible odds, and they knew that as long as they stood together, they could overcome any obstacle and continue to make a difference in the world.

The battle for Veridan's soul had been won, but the fight for justice and truth would continue. And Alex and Sarah were ready to face whatever challenges lay ahead, driven by their shared commitment to making the world a better place.

Don't miss out!

Visit the website below and you can sign up to receive emails whenever Nicholas Andrew Martinez publishes a new book. There's no charge and no obligation.

https://books2read.com/r/B-A-HUIXB-PDXIF

BOOKS2READ

Connecting independent readers to independent writers.

About the Author

Nicholas Andrew Martinez is a distinguished author known for his gripping political fiction. His novels delve into the intricacies of power, corruption, and intrigue, offering readers a thrilling and insightful look at the political landscape. With a background in political science and a passion for storytelling, Martinez crafts narratives that are both thought-provoking and suspenseful. Outside of writing, he enjoys analyzing current events, traveling, and engaging in civic discussions. Nicholas's work continues to captivate and challenge readers, cementing his reputation as a leading voice in political fiction.